BY
ROBERT MAYER

 St. Martin's Griffin ♔ New York

For Carol

Lyrics from "The Middle Class (Le Bourgeois)" by Jacques Brel, translated by Eric Blau, used by permission of Bagatelle Editions Musicales, Paris.

Book design by Jack Ribik

www.stmartins.com

Library of Congress Cataloging-in-Publication Data

Mayer, Robert, 1939–
Superfolks.

ISBN: 978-0-312-33992-0
ISBN: 0-312-33992-5

I. Title.
PZ4.M4692Su [PS3563.A954]
813'.5'4   76-53033

First published in the United States by The Dial Press

P 1

Foreword

I'd been writing comics for money for more than ten years when I first heard about this mythical, inspirational *Superfolks* book, but none of the local stores knew what I was talking about when I went looking for the damned, elusive thing. In the end, someone finally palmed me a battered U.K. paperback edition, with a cover painting of a morose, chubby man in spandex. There he was, slumped by a miserable yellow table light, as if all wonder, all hope and joy had been leached from his useless life. It didn't look like much but I'd heard good things and the idea of a prose writer tackling superhero comic "themes" in a semi-serious manner was enough of a novelty for me to give it a go.

Behind the unpromising pulp facade, I was happy to uncover some of the aboriginal roots nourishing the '80s "adult" superhero comic boom. I've always enjoyed tracking the developing fashions and styles of comic book writing and art across our branching tree of influences and progenitors, and in *Superfolks* I'd found a barely acknowledged contribution to the vivid and explosive evolution of the "mature" superhero story that characterized the '80s and '90s. Here, too, by extension, can be found one of the throbbing taproots of the latest vogue for black-humored, violent, and controversial cape dramas. In his bittersweet portrayal of the middle-aged Captain Mantra, with that half-remembered magic word always hovering somewhere on the tip of his tongue, I could see that Robert Mayer had prefigured the era of so-called "deconstructionist" superheroes, which in turn spawned many of the medium's most memorable and ambitious works. In the conspiracy themes, complex twisting plotlines, fifth-dimensional science, thrilling set pieces, and reverses of *Superfolks*, we can almost sniff the soil that grew so many of our favorite comics in the '80s, '90s, and beyond. In its wicked humor, we hear the ironic sneer of a whole new generation of comic book writers and their successors. Historians of the funnies will find in *Superfolks* a treasure trove of tropes. Everyone else gets a good laugh and a good story as Mayer takes us to a wonky Earth-Nil parallel universe of downtrodden urban supermen and clapped-out cartoons. Back in the day when comic book heroes were mostly still innocent of the ravages of time and cynicism, these fallen, fallible men and women of clay must have seemed monstrous parodies. Now they'd fit right in with the locals in any comic book universe. These days no one would be able to know how to tell the joke from the real thing.

With much to recommend it to scholars and casual readers alike, it's way past time *Superfolks* had a chance to shine for a wider audience. As super-superheroes replace cowboys, detectives, and spacemen on our screens, in our hearts, our minds, and imaginations, there's always room for a note of caution, humanity, and mocking laughter in the dark. This is a daft and beautiful little jewel of a book and should be savored like silly wine. It would, in fact, make a very good film, Hollywood-san.

Oh, and Mister Mayer, you really should be writing some comics yourself. Our heroes have finally caught up with you. I think they can handle it.

Ladies and gentlemen, *Superfolks* by Robert Mayer . . .

Grant Morrison
Glasgow, Scotland, August 2004

**Behold, I teach you the Superman:
he is this lightning, he is this madness!**

—Friedrich Wilhelm Nietzsche
Thus Spake Zarathustra

There were no more heroes.

Kennedy was dead, shot by an assassin in Dallas.

Batman and Robin were dead, killed when the Batmobile slammed into a bus carrying black children to school in the suburbs.

Superman was missing, and presumed dead, after a Kryptonite meteor fell on Metropolis.

The Marvel family was dead; struck down by lightning.

The Lone Ranger was dead; found with an arrow in his back after Tonto returned from a Red Power conference at Wounded Knee.

Mary Mantra was dead; cut to pieces by an Amtrak locomotive when Dr. Spock tied her to the tracks and she couldn't remove her gag.

Captain Mantra was in a sanitarium near Edgeville; said to be a helpless wretch ever since seeing his twin sister cut to shreds.

Only Wonder Woman was still in the public eye. And she had forsworn forever the use of her superpowers. Using her real name, Diana Prince, she was a leading spokesperson for women's liberation, an associate editor of *Ms.* magazine, a frequent guest on late-night talk shows. Her message was that the strength of Wonder Woman resides in all women and they must learn to use it. Battling to liberate womankind, she said, was more important than catching petty crooks. She sounded at times like a sinner repentant.

Even Snoopy had bought it; shot down by the Red Baron; missing in action over France.

In this fading pantheon of heroes, the very last to give up combat against the forces of tyranny and evil had been the most powerful hero of all. And he had not been seen in almost a decade. Not since, unknown to the world, his superpowers had unaccountably begun to fail.

Using his secret identity, David Brinkley, he had slipped into the humdrum routine of middle-class life. He was forty-two years old. He was married, with two children; and a third was due any day. He expected never again to dash into a phone booth, strip down to his uniform, don his purple mask, and leap into battle against the forces of darkness.

He had outgrown such childish notions. They lived on only in his dreams.

So he thought.

His six-foot-one-inch frame was slumped in a brown-leather easy chair, his legs resting on a hassock. He was wearing a beige turtleneck, brown slacks, brown and beige argyle socks, HushPuppies. He had blue hair.

His black horn-rimmed glasses were perched on the bridge of his nose. Years ago the glasses had been part of a disguise, and were fitted with clear plastic. Now they contained prescription lenses.

Light from the color-television screen mingled with smoke from his cigar, creating ghosts. The dog, a golden retriever, leaped at the empty air, snarling; and landed heavily.

"Bernstein!" he shouted; and shoved the dog away with his foot.

The dog was eight years old. Punch Rosenthal had given it to him when David gave up broadcasting and returned to the newspaper. Punch had gotten a good laugh when he heard the name. Punch hated *West Side Story*.

In truth, Brinkley had named the dog after the Everett Sloane character in *Citizen Kane;* one of his Top-Three movies. His favorite scene was when Bernstein recalls the girl in the white raincoat. At forty-two, Brinkley was still a romantic; a prisoner of illusion. Though in recent years his view of the world had started to change. Justice did not always triumph. Happy endings were not necessarily the rule.

The commercial for Preparation H ended. The asshole dissolved on the screen. The Monday-night football game was about to resume. Oakland was coming out of its huddle, advancing to the line of scrimmage. Brinkley leaned forward in his chair, the cigar clenched in his teeth. Oakland was leading Kansas City by three points. With thirty seconds to play, Oakland had the ball on the Kansas City nine-yard line. Oakland needed a touchdown to reach the point-spread of nine. If they didn't score, Brinkley would owe Freddie News another twenty bucks. That would make two hundred and fifty bucks he owed Freddie News, between the World Series and the half-eaten football season. Freddie News was stealing the braces off Allison Brinkley's teeth.

The dog was chewing the toe of Brinkley's left HushPuppy. Brinkley let him chew. It was better than the dog pissing on his leg.

In Brinkley's dreams lately, the dog was often pissing on his leg.

Oakland was at the line of scrimmage, the quarterback calling signals. Brinkley held his breath. All over Middleville, men were leaning forward, holding their breaths. Waiting to see if Oakland would make the point-spread.

The screen went dark. The football field was replaced by a blue-and-white sign. The sign said BULLETIN.

"Damn!" he said.

All over Middleville, an echo answered: DAMN!

A faceless announcer was intoning:

LADIES AND GENTLEMEN, WE INTERRUPT THIS BROADCAST TO BRING YOU A BULLETIN FROM ABC NEWS.

"Thirty seconds," Brinkley spat at the screen, taking the cigar from his mouth. "Fucking bulletin couldn't wait half a minute?"

WE SWITCH YOU NOW TO OUR STUDIOS IN NEW YORK.

"Another Heidi!" Brinkley said, addressing the screen again.

He noticed that the room was heavy with blue smoke. Since the "heart attack," as the doctors had mistakenly called it, he had given up cigars, for appearance' sake. He allowed himself only one a week, during the Monday-night football game; when Pamela was away at her consciousness-raising group.

THIS IS BILL BEUTEL IN NEW YORK. TURMOIL BORDERING ON ANARCHY HAS BROKEN OUT IN THIS CITY TONIGHT. LOOTERS HAVE SMASHED WINDOWS OF HUNDREDS OF DOWNTOWN STORES. MUGGINGS HAVE BEEN REPORTED THROUGHOUT THE MIDTOWN AREA. IN THE THREE HOURS SINCE SUNDOWN, NINE RAPES HAVE BEEN REPORTED IN CENTRAL PARK ALONE.

OFFICIALS FEAR THAT THE EXPLOSION OF STREET INCIDENTS IS THE BEGINNING OF THE CHAOS THEY PREDICTED WHEN NEW YORK WENT BANKRUPT TWO MONTHS AGO.

LAST WEEK THE CITY'S ENTIRE THIRTY-THOUSAND-MAN POLICE FORCE RESIGNED, AFTER WORKING WITH NO PAY FOR SEVEN WEEKS. THE MEN WERE GIVEN JOBS WITH LEADING INDUSTRIAL FIRMS SO THEY COULD SUPPORT THEIR FAMILIES. BUT THAT LEFT THE CITY WITH NO POLICE PROTECTION.

FOR THE PAST WEEK CALM HAS PREVAILED IN THE CITY. BUT ALL THAT APPEARS TO HAVE CHANGED TONIGHT. THE CRIES OF VICTIMS OF STABBINGS AND BLUDGEONINGS PIERCE THE DOWNTOWN NIGHT. CITY HOSPITALS ARE FILLED. THE NATIONAL GUARD IS BEING MOBILIZED. AT THIS HOUR CITY AND STATE OFFICIALS ARE MEETING TO DISCUSS THE CRISIS. ONE HIGH OFFICIAL TOLD ME JUST MOMENTS AGO: "IT'S THE DARNDEST THING I'VE EVER SEEN. IT'S ALMOST AS IF THE WHOLE THING WAS ORGANIZED."

ACCORDING TO THE ASSOCIATED PRESS, SEVERAL

EYEWITNESSES HAVE SWORN THAT THE ATTACKERS COULD NOT BE HUMAN; THAT HUMAN BEINGS WOULDN'T ACT THAT WAY. BUT WHEN PRESSED FOR DETAILS, THEY COULD NOT PINPOINT ANY DIFFERENCE.

THIS IS BILL BEUTEL IN NEW YORK. STAY TUNED TO ABC NEWS FOR FURTHER REPORTS.

The BULLETIN sign faded from the screen. The football field returned. Both teams were running toward the sidelines. The camera showed the face of a smiling coach.

"Not a great football game, but a good football game," Howard Cosell was saying. "Don't forget next Monday night, it's the Jets at Miami. That one is always a bruiser. This is Howard Cosell saying . . ."

"Dammit, what was the score?" Brinkley said aloud.

". . . we'll see you all next week. The final score once again: Oakland twenty-four, Kansas City twenty-one."

"Son of a bitch," he said.

The screen faded to a commercial for Odor Eaters. Brinkley shoved the hassock away with his foot. He eased up out of the chair, and snapped off the set. The knob came off in his hand.

He looked at the knob, puzzled. That hadn't happened for years.

Middleville was a playpen suburb forty miles from New York, on the north shore of Swansdown Island. The island stretched pickle-shaped for eighty miles from the city into the sea, and was pocked with suburban communities. Edgeville, the closest to the city, had the most prestige and the most expensive homes, with clandestine affairs and preening sailboats attached. From its rolling, shaded hills the towers of Manhattan could be seen across the South River. Beyond Edgeville the land gradually flattened, and was covered, in turn, by Nearville, Fairville, Floralville, Gardenville, Oakville, Pleasantville, Vistaville, Sunnyville, Strongville, Roseville, Middleville, Townville, Ladyville, Robinville, Flatville, Spudville, Branchville, Farville, Tideville, Oceanville, and Parsons Corners.

After Edgeville, the suburbs all looked like mechanical drawings; except for Parsons Corners on the tip of the island, which was still a rural community of potato fields and red barns and silver silos and cows being milked at six o'clock in the morning; not unlike Littletown, in the northern part of the state, where Brinkley had lived as a boy.

Most of the inhabitants of Swansdown Island had grown up in the streets and alleys and brick tenements of the city, and had moved to the suburbs after their children were born. The only people who still lived in New York were Negroes, Puerto Ricans, artists, writers, Eli Wallach, old people waiting for death, and the ultra-rich.

The rich people of Edgeville thought that they ruled the world. The ultra-rich of New York *knew* that *they* ruled the world; and they exhibited a serene confidence and devotion to the arts born of that knowledge.

The world actually was ruled by a shadowy, rarely seen Dallas multi-billionaire midget named Powell Pugh.

In the family room of his colonial-style house in Middleville, Brinkley studied the television knob in his hand, and replaced it on the set. He was feeling irritated. He told himself he was annoyed because Oakland had failed to score; because he had lost twenty more bucks to Freddie News. He knew that was only part of the reason. With each passing moment the BULLETIN was worming deeper into his brain. It seemed to contain some hidden invitation; some scarcely veiled threat.

He tried to dismiss the thought. He crossed to the wall cabinet, and turned on the stereo. The Jacques Brel show was on the turntable, from the night before. One of his Top-Three musicals. The last show he had taken dear old screwed-up Peggy to, years ago. The robot arm settled onto the record, the room was filled with the sound of dust. Then the opening chorus. He turned the volume down low, so as not to wake the children.

No matter what happened in the city, Pamela and the children would be safe. Anarchy would never come to Middleville. That was what suburbs were all about. But was that credo enough to illuminate his remaining thirty years? Had he survived the destruction of another world . . . for this?

Why not, he asked himself. He owed nothing to anybody. The promise of his childhood—his immortality—had not been kept. He was growing old.

He looked at the electric digital clock that was spouting sunbursts on the bookcase; sunbursts like planets exploding. It was 10:02. As he watched, another planet erupted. It was 10:03. Pamela would not be home from her women's group for an hour yet.

He remembered a small incident that had occurred the night

long ago when he and Peggy saw the Brel show. He had gone into the street during intermission, for a smoke. Peggy had gone to the ladies' room. There was a bar next to the theater, and people were crowded around the television set. The ten o'clock news had a direct hookup to La Guardia Airport, where a large jet was circling overhead in a holding pattern; unable to land because an engine was on fire and might cause an explosion on impact. Ambulances and emergency vehicles were being rushed to the field. Firemen were covering the runway with foam. He had hurried into the men's room of the bar, slipped into a toilet stall, and left his clothes on a hook. Seconds later he was streaking out the window toward the airport. He found the plane easily in the night sky. Using his superbreath, he blew out the flames. He signaled the pilot to lower the landing gear and cut the engines. When that was done he stretched his body under the fuselage, his arms spread wide, and carried the plane on his back to a perfect landing. There were ninety-nine people aboard. Every one of them was cheering as he hauled the disabled plane to the terminal. (One of them was John Wayne.) He did not wait around for thanks. He streaked back to the bar, climbed in through the window, and put on his clothes. He slipped into his seat just as the second act was beginning.

Peggy had asked where he had been. Stomach cramps, he said.

Dear dead days of his greatness.

And now . . . now he did not even know if he could handle muggers in the streets.

He went into the kitchen, and opened the stuffed refrigerator, looking for something to eat. He closed it again, quickly. The Mallomars he ate on the copy desk every day were winning out over his weekly tennis game. Already he was ten pounds over his best flying weight.

He crushed the thought, fiercely. He had no flying weight. He had not flown—really flown—in eight years. Not since his superpowers had begun to ebb, for no reason that he could discover.

They had moved from Manhattan to Middleville shortly

after Allison was born. He had given up reporting, and become an editor on the day copy desk, making corrections and writing headlines. It would be a quieter life, with more time to spend with his family.

At about the same time, his appearances in the skies over New York had become fewer and fewer; until they had stopped altogether.

The crime rate—most notably the corruption of public officials—had risen dramatically soon after.

At first the people of the city assumed he was away catching muggers in other galaxies; and would soon return. But as the months became years, they began to accept the unthinkable.

For a long time, he himself had not been able to do that. His inexplicable weakness colored his every waking moment—and often his nightmares as well. It was not supposed to be.

He had been born on the planet Cronk. There was only one substance in the entire universe to which he was supposed to be vulnerable: Cronkite. He had learned early in his supercareer to retreat quickly when villains brought lumps of Cronkite into his presence. But this other, gradual, all-pervasive weakness he couldn't understand.

There had been nothing to do but accept his fate. He thought of his former exploits less and less—except late at night, when Pamela was asleep, and he lay staring into the darkness, and could feel again the wind in his cape, and the tingle in his fist when he klunked a villain on the jaw, a helpless eeyargh! escaping the villain's throat. When he wished he were young again.

Last night, for instance. He had been remembering the time his telepathic powers warned him that a giant tidal wave as tall as the Empire State Building was rolling toward the city. He had dived into the water and dug a three-mile-deep channel the length of the city. The channel absorbed the entire wave. Not an extra drop of water rolled up onto the beach at Coney Island.

The people of the city had never even known of the danger. But his fellow heroes knew. Telegrams of congratulation had poured in from around the world: from Wonder Woman on Paradise Island; from Batman in Gotham; from Superman in Metropolis; from the Lone Ranger in Albuquerque.

He had won two Golden Apollos that year at the annual Pantheon Award ceremonies on Saturn: Best Feat Using Telepathic Powers, and Best Feat Under Water. And he hadn't even campaigned.

But that had been years ago. Now he was living in Middleville, his telepathic powers gone, his superstrength becoming puny; almost mortal. His mind and body approaching middle age.

And like a searing blowtorch, the BULLETIN from the city was firing the dead past.

He crossed the dining room with its colonial table, and peered into the living room. Points of stray light gleamed from the polished furniture like lost ideals. The Brinkleys did not live in the living room; they lived in the family room. No one in all of Middleville lived in the living room.

On the phonograph, Elly Stone was concluding Brel's tribute to past love: *Yet you see, I've forgotten your name*

> *your name*
> *your name*
> *your name*
> *your name*

He moved to the cabinet, lifted the needle out of the scratch in the record, set it down farther along. Then he switched off the set. He needed to focus his attention; to forget the BULLETIN. He decided to pay some bills.

He climbed the carpeted stairs to the upper hallway. He looked in on Allison, who was sleeping on her stomach, her small face pressed sideways to the pillow; and on Jennifer, who was on her back, sucking her thumb. They were pretty children, with Pamela's soft blonde hair and his own dark eyes. He was grateful for that. He had been afraid they would inherit his blue hair.

He entered the master bedroom and sat down at his desk in the corner. He pulled the current bills out of the middle drawer, and riffled through them. Three hundred and six dollars due on Master Charge. Eighty-eight dollars on the Gulf Oil card. A payment due on the station wagon. Fifty-two dollars from Bloomingdale's (the lowest in a year; Pamela was "being good"). Thirty-six dollars from Swansdown Light and Power (along with a booklet on electricity for the Eskimos). A mortgage payment due on the house. (Twenty-three more years and it would be his.) A hundred and fifty for Dr. Sikes, though the baby wasn't born yet. A request from the United Way. A request from the American Cancer Society. (Cancer of the colon was the Cancer-of-the-Month.) A request from the Powell Pugh Foundation.

He couldn't concentrate. He placed his checkbook and the bills back in the drawer. He went down to the kitchen, and pulled on the yellow rubber gloves. Pamela would expect the dishes done when she got home.

He squeezed a few drops of Joy onto a sponge. (Once, years ago, he had squeezed the throat of Univac in similar fashion, and saved the world.) He caught sight of his face in the window above the sink: square-jawed, square-cheeked, clear as a comic strip. There was no hint of uncertainty in it.

To find the fears, the conflicts, the frustrations, you had to look inside. He was worried about how they would pay all their bills, with inflation eating away his salary, and the baby coming. He was bored with his job; he did not like going to an office every day; he wanted to be his own boss, but did not know what else he could do. He was beginning to feel his years in his bones, and wondered what earthly diseases he was now susceptible to. His family was an island of calm; but an island in a sea of boredom. There was no excitement in his life anymore, no challenge, no commitment to anything beyond himself. It left a void somewhere deep inside him. And now, at the wrong time, with the baby due any day, his conscience was beginning to stir. His conscience was a troublemaker from way back.

It's the darndest thing I've ever seen. It's almost as if the whole thing was organized.

A passing remark—or an invitation? A casual comment—or quicksand? Quicksand that would suck him down, suck him back . . . though he wasn't fit . . . though he couldn't handle it.

Suddenly he got cold feet. He looked away from the window, down into the sink. The running water had overflowed the sinkful of dishes. The water was pouring over the cupboard and onto the Kentile floor. His HushPuppies were soaked. Bernstein was licking at floating bits of spaghetti.

He reached over and turned off the water.

"Son of a bitch," he said.

Just then, as if on schedule, the telephone rang.

—

The topless dancer called herself Bermuda Triangle. She had auburn hair, and a bored expression. Her breasts were shaped like Florida. There were gleaming silver pasties over Miami.

She was gyrating in the smoky spotlight of the Mafia Club, on the East Side of Manhattan. The arc of the spotlight illuminated the shoes of the three-piece combo behind her. The drummer rolled his drums. Bermuda Triangle shimmied her shoulder blades.

"Dig that action!" Gimp said. "They go in different directions."

The Mafia Club was known to the organized-crime section of the police department—when there was a police department—as a hangout for the mob. Gimp had never been there before. He was a new recruit.

He was seated at a small table in the rear. He was wearing the only suit he owned, dark blue, and the only white shirt he owned. He did not own a tie. His crutch was leaning against the wall beside him. He was drinking his fourth beer; and hoping that Peppy would pick up the check.

Peppy would.

Gimp had not met Peppy before tonight. He had never met anyone like Peppy before. Peppy, seated with his back to the wall, exuded power, though he was only four feet tall, and he dressed like a dandy. He was wearing a purple velvet suit and vest, a white shirt, and a green bow tie, and had a purple bowler and a gold-handled walking stick on the seat beside him. He had a bald head, and a nose that curved upward, like an elf. He was drinking white wine. Gimp had never tasted white wine.

"Gentlemen, a toast," Peppy said, raising his glass, "before we thay good-bye."

Gimp raised his glass of beer. Stretch raised his vodka-tonic. Stretch was the third man at the table. He was a regular at the Mafia Club. He had recruited Gimp; had introduced him to Peppy. He was tall and thin, sallow, rubber-faced, an El Greco image in a red and black checked sports jacket and a yellow shirt.

"To the beginning . . . of the end," Peppy said. He spoke slowly, in a high-pitched voice, over the pounding drums, savoring each phrase as if it were champagne. "To the beginning . . . of the end . . . of Indigo."

The men clinked glasses, and drank.

"Do you think he'll show tomorrow?" Stretch said, setting his glass on the table.

Peppy smiled. "He'll show," he said. "Thooner or later. Meanwhile, you know what to do. Tomorrow night you thend twice as many . . . men . . . into action. Where the National Guard is thin." He turned to Gimp. "You know what to do in the morning?"

Gimp nodded.

"Then I'm off," Peppy said.

He stood. The others did not immediately realize that he had stood. He took a roll of bills from his pocket, and tossed a twenty onto the table. The others stood in deference as he maneuvered out of the room like a skinny penguin in a purple hat, past a small table where Mario Puzo and Gay Talese were drinking bourbon.

A black limousine was waiting for him at the curb, with the motor running. The driver was also a bodyguard, but he had been told he would not need a gun on this assignment. He missed the heft of steel in his belt. He felt vaguely unpatriotic.

Peppy told the driver to take him to the hotel. He also told him to call ahead, so they would have a young boy waiting.

Inside, the white spotlight had turned purple. Bermuda Triangle, her pasties gone, writhed slowly in the heavy light, as if she were under water. Joe Bambi, who owned the Mafia Club, moved through the tables in a tuxedo, and squeezed Stretch's shoulder. Joe Bambi was Vito Corelli's underboss. Vito Corelli ran the mob in New York.

"Who's the dude?" Bambi said.

"You don't know him?"

"He's not my type."

"Name's Peppy," Stretch said. "He's from out of town."

"What's he got that we want?"

"Bread. Acres and acres of bread."

"You workin' on somethin'?"

Stretch nodded; and finished his drink. He enjoyed knowing something Bambi didn't. It ate Bambi up.

"Corelli know about this?" Bambi said.

"Of course Corelli knows. You think I mix with guys like that? He's from another world. He's a personal friend of Corelli's. He approached Corelli direct."

Stretch did not have to curry favor with Joe Bambi by telling him anything. Stretch was not exactly a member of the family. His last name was O'Toole.

The music stopped. The stage went dark. Dim lights brightened throughout the room. The dancer was gone, like a vanished illusion. The stage was bare wooden planking.

Gimp was bored. His bad leg was beginning to ache.

"Got to visit with my customers," Bambi said, irritated. "Take care of yourself."

He moved off to another table, where Frank Sinatra, Spiro Agnew and two blonde ladies were having a raucous conversation over sirloin steaks.

"Let's go," Stretch said.

He handed Gimp his crutch, and a cardboard box from

under the table, and helped him through the bar and out the door. Between the crutch, the pain and the beers, Gimp was swaying like a toy ship in swelling seas.

Stretch flagged a cab at the curb.

"You know why that broad calls herself Bermuda Triangle?" Gimp said. His voice was thick with beer.

"No. Why?"

"Because so many men have gone down there."

Stretch was impressed. He hadn't thought Gimp was that bright.

Gimp climbed awkwardly into the taxi, clutching the box, pulling his crutch in after him.

"You know what to do in the morning?" Stretch asked.

"Stop worrying," Gimp said.

Stretch closed the door. The cab pulled away. He turned, and went back into the club, and sat at the leatherette bar. Bermuda Triangle, wearing a green satin dress, sat beside him; and rubbed his thigh with her hand. Bermuda would go home with Stretch O'Toole after work anytime he wanted. She loved his long, lean body, his rubbery limbs; his infinite . . . possibilities.

His HushPuppies made squee-
gee sounds as he crossed the kitchen. He lifted the wall receiver.
Water from his rubber glove ran down his arm to his elbow.

"Hello?"

"Hello, David? This is Punch."

He recognized the voice immediately, though Punch hadn't
called him at home in years. Once he had been Punch's blue-
haired boy. Punch had grown up in North Carolina, was a frus-
trated novelist, and liked any young man who could "write a
good lick." In those days Brinkley used to write a good lick.
For years he had been the paper's ace reporter. Then a commen-
tator with NBC. Now he was just another old China hand.
Punch had new blue-haired boys.

"Hi, Punch."

He still felt like a small boy when talking to Punch Rosenthal; felt an undercurrent of guilt, as if in some way he never
quite had lived up to Punch's expectations; or his own.

"How are you, David? How's the family?"

The voice was preoccupied, formal. Punch didn't care much
anymore.

"Fine. Pamela's due any day now."

"That's right, I almost forgot. Let's hope it's a boy this
time.

"Doesn't matter," he lied.

Once, Punch had been one of his Top-Three people. Not anymore. Sometimes Brinkley's life seemed strewn with used-up relationships; rusty friendships abandoned in a field, lying at odd angles in the rain. A failure to keep the contact points clean; to guard against emotional crud.

"I'm calling about business, sort of. Have you heard the news?"

"About the city? I saw a bulletin."

"It's worse than that. The National Guard is out. Things are quiet now, but it's gonna get worse. I can smell it. There's something really rotten going on. There are things they aren't saying on the tube."

"Like what?"

"I don't want to go into it now. I'll tell you in the office."

"You want me to come in tonight? You need an extra man on the desk?"

"No, things are under control right now. Actually, it's not you I'm calling about. It's . . ."

He knew. Even before the word was spoken. His heart began flying in his breast.

"If my hunch is right, this thing is going to unravel until only he can get to the bottom of it."

"But he's . . . retired, or whatever. Nobody's seen him in eight years. Some people say he's dead. Besides . . . what does that have to do with me?"

He held his breath, waiting for the response. He didn't know what he would do if Punch knew. He wasn't even sure it mattered anymore. That was the worst part.

"David, you were his best friend."

"Well, one of them, anyway."

He let his breath out slowly.

"Do you think he's dead?"

"I . . . I don't know. . . . Not that I know of."

"Well, I don't either. I don't know where he is, or what he's been up to. I suppose he has his reasons. But New York needs him now."

"What is it you expect me to do?"

"I want you to try to contact him, somehow. He must have left some message, some clue, some way of getting in touch with him. Didn't he?"

For eight years, in some buried part of his brain, Brinkley had suspected that one day a call like this would come. Still, he was not prepared. He didn't know what to say. He needed time to think. He said nothing.

"Think back. There must have been something. If you think of it, let me know. Or get in touch with him yourself. It doesn't matter. As long as we reach him before things get out of hand."

His palms were perspiring in the sticky gloves.

"Punch, I know your hunches are usually right. But are you sure everybody isn't overreacting to a couple of muggings? As soon as the police go back to work . . . ."

"Listen to me. The National Guard has picked up some of these muggers. They're not the same kind of people as you and I."

"Punch, blacks are people, too."

"This is serious."

"I'm sorry."

"We all may be sorry unless we can locate him."

"And what if he really is dead?"

"Then we're in big trouble. Let me know how you make out. I've got an edition to get out."

There was silence on the line.

"Good night, David."

"Good night, Punch."

He hung up the receiver. He pulled off the rubber gloves, and tossed them onto the counter. His hands smelled faintly putrid.

He left the mess in the kitchen, and sank into the leather easy chair in the family room. His retreat. His castle.

He could picture the bustle in the city room at the paper. Punch in his glassed-in office, the sleeves of his white shirt rolled up, his tie loosened, his large white head bent over his desk, dummying a new front page for the second edition. Arthur Gold, the city editor, taking calls from reporters with a phone at each ear, buzzing Punch on the intercom with the latest developments. Bob Mayer, the bright kid right out of journalism school, at the front rewrite desk, doing the main story. John Corry hovering nearby, feeding him color he had picked up on the streets. Pete Hamill retopping his column. Gorman on the picture desk screaming for his pictures from the photo lab. Zombie, the aging copyboy, hand-running (hand-walking) copy to the back shop. The wires clattering in the corner. Racquel, the cute new copygirl with the big tits, bringing coffee and sandwiches from the cafeteria, gripped with excitement; the same excitement that had lured him from Littletown to the big city.

That afternoon he himself had edited a book review, a movie review, and a feature for the Sunday paper on how to get the best results with a Cuisinart.

He pulled off his wet shoes. He stood, and paced the room in his argyle socks. He didn't know what to do.

If Punch was right, if there was big trouble brewing, then he ought to get help. But who? There was nobody left. He was alone. Alone in Middleville. Alone in the universe.

He watched a planet exploding on the digital clock. He could tell Punch that he couldn't locate him. He could tell him that he was dead. That would put an end to it, once and for all. Mankind would be put on notice. It would have to look after itself. Perhaps that was the kindest thing he could do, in the long run.

Another sunburst splintered on the clock. He saw in his mind's eye the planet Cronk erupting, exploding. Saw a man and a woman, Archie and Edith, placing an infant boy in a rocket, firing the baby toward Earth, to be a savior. Saw the man and the woman being consumed by flame. As in some primal nightmare.

He remained motionless for many seconds. Paying homage. Then he reached down, and picked up his wet shoes. Adrenalin was swimming in his blood. He let the dog outside, and went upstairs.

The uniform was packed in a cardboard box marked Photographs, at the back of the top of the bedroom closet, beneath hat boxes, torn sheets, a broken vacuum cleaner, and slipcovers for a couch they had given to the Salvation Army while they still lived in Manhattan. He stood on the chair from his desk, burrowed through the junk, and with difficulty managed to pull out the box. It was covered with dust. The dust filled his nostrils. He started to sneeze, and lost his balance. He just managed to land on his feet as the chair tumbled out from under him.

He carried the box to the bathroom and wiped it with toilet paper. Then he placed it carefully on the bed, and pulled off the top. Dozens of brown and gray photographs spilled over the edges. Some were of Pamela as a little girl, her hair in braids. Most were of himself as a boy in Littletown: in the arms of Mother after they found him in the rocket ship; in his baseball uniform with the number 00 on the back, years after they had adopted him from the orphanage to which they first had taken him; playing croquet with Father on the back lawn; standing with the guys on the steps of Littletown High; clowning in front of the drugstore; five boys and five girls around a white-colored table at the senior prom, the girls wearing strapless dresses and corsages, the boys wearing white jackets and black bow ties. Seated next to him was his date, Lorna Doone.

For the most part, a typical American childhood. With no pictures of the other. No one ever knew the real him. No one ever would.

He often longed for the purposelessness of other men: to earn, to play, to breed, to die; without reason. With no creative mission. With no need to save the world.

Of late he had fashioned such a life for himself. And found he hated it. His muscles were chafing the insides of his skin. He had become boring; to himself most of all. Waves of anxiety shuddered through him at unexpected moments, for no visible reason. He was afraid that one day soon he would lose his mind.

Perhaps, then, this plea from the city—though it made him tremble—had been sent by the gods. An answer to unspoken prayers. A kick at dream-dogs pissing on his legs.

He shoved the photographs aside. Beneath them was tissue paper. Inside the paper was the uniform. (He and Pamela had met at a masquerade party. If she ever found the uniform, he would say it was from another masquerade, long ago. But she had never found it.)

His heart thumped recklessly as he lifted the uniform out of the box, carefully, piece by piece: the skin-tight blue leotards, with his emblem in white on the chest; the slim red boots; the red overshorts; the white cape; the purple mask. A warmth akin to love pervaded him; as if he had encountered a dear, lost friend.

He found himself shaking as he pulled the turtleneck over his head, and opened his belt, and pulled off his pants. With trepidation, he slipped into the skin-tight blues. He had expected the worst; he thought they wouldn't fit at all. He was pleasantly surprised. They were tight, he had extra rolls of flesh at his stomach and his belly that hadn't been there in the old days, but the taut material acted as a corset, pulling him in. It wasn't comfortable, but it would do.

He pulled up the overshorts, and belted them, a feat made possible by his tucked-in belly. The boots presented no problem. He fastened the cape around his shoulders, and, still trembling, opened the closet door, and looked at his image in the full-length mirror.

His chest swelled several inches at the sight of himself. It wasn't bad. It wasn't bad at all.

The Man of Iron!

The Man of Tomorrow!

He smiled, and snorted, and let the air out of his chest.

"The man of yesterday," he said.

He paced the room, restless. He needed to test his powers; to see how badly they had deteriorated during the last few years. To see what he still could do. To see if he would be of any use at all.

He put on his purple mask. Impulsively, he turned. And dove toward the window.

There was a crash of glass, as first his hands and then his shoulders hit. He had forgotten to open it.

The glass clattered on the patio below. His momentum was gone, and he couldn't clear the maple tree outside. He crashed into the silhouette of browning leaves. He tried to fall lightly to the ground. But his cape snagged on a protruding branch. He was left dangling from the tree in the darkness, his feet yards off the ground. Bernstein came racing around from the front of the house, and began leaping and barking at his swaying ankles.

"Creeping Cronkite!" Brinkley said.

In his mind, he had said, "Son of a bitch." But whenever he was in uniform, his epithets came out something dumb, like "Creeping Cronkite." Something with a PG rating. That much, at least, was still the same.

A light went on in an upstairs window across the street. The window opened, and a perfectly bald head appeared in it, like a full moon in eclipse.

"What's going on out there?" a nasty voice yelled.

It was Kojak, his neighbor. Kojak was a cop in the city. Or had been, until he had resigned with all the others a week ago. They didn't like each other much. Kojak had no use for what he called the "weeping media,"

Brinkley hung motionless in the shadow of the tree. He

focused his gamma-eye vision on the streetlight twenty yards away. He waited, straining; as if constipated. He couldn't believe nothing was happening. Then, after several seconds, it worked. The heat from his vision caused the tungsten to flare. The bulb burned out. He was cloaked in darkness.

"It's all right, Kojak," he yelled. "It's me."

"Brinkley? That you? What the hell is goin' on?"

Bernstein was still barking. He felt like a fool, dangling from the tree.

"It's okay," he yelled. "It's just the dog. He was chasing a ball. He broke a window."

"Well, shut the damn pooch up, baby. There's people tryin' to sleep."

The bald moon retracted into the window, like the head of a turtle. The window slammed down. The light went out.

The dog kept barking.

"Shut up," he whispered fiercely.

He tensed his stomach muscles, and swung his legs over his head, till his feet found footing on a thick branch. From there he managed to free his twisted cape. He dropped to the ground.

The dog was on him in an instant, snarling. He grabbed the jaws with his hands, and clamped them shut.

"Bernstein!" he said.

He was about to hit him, when he realized what the trouble was. The dog had never seen him in this getup.

He leaned his face low, so the dog could smell him and know who it was. Then he let go of the jaws. The dog licked his face in a wide swatch, his tongue dripping with saliva.

"Creeping Cronkite!" he said again.

Staying in the shadows, he moved to the front of the house to put the dog inside. The door was locked. He didn't have his key.

That was one thing about the uniform that was a pain in the ass. There were no pockets.

The dog calmed down, and bounded off to sniff the broken glass. Brinkley sat on the front step, chagrined. It was just nervousness, he told himself. If he had remembered to open the window, it might have been all right.

He had to try again.

He stood, muscles tensing. Butterflies the size of eagles danced in his belly. Running backs must feel this way, he thought, waiting for the opening kickoff.

He placed his arms high above his head, like a child learning to dive. He let good thoughts drift easily into his head.

He leaped. And found he was already in the air, climbing, climbing. Above the rooftop. Above the treetop. Rising gently, almost effortlessly, into the moonless night. Climbing higher. Feeling stronger as he climbed. Higher. Higher still. The tenseness fell away, replaced by exultation. Lightness returned to his body. Gladness to his heart.

"Jonathan Livingston Me," he said to the passing air, and couldn't repress a smile.

He swooped left and headed west, toward MacArthur Park two miles away. Over the dark expanse of park, deserted at night, there was less chance he would be seen. He reached the park, still climbing. He let himself drift. Slowly he changed position, and flew straight up. Then he did a flip, and darted straight down. Not too fast, nothing fancy. Just testing.

The old exuberance was returning. The old self-confidence. Here over the park the years seemed to melt away. The air offered no resistance. The world was at his feet; just as it used to be.

He had always been most at home up in the air. On earth he could not make total contact with another person; could never communicate the core of his existence, the reason for his being, the strength inside the weakness—or the weakness inside the strength—he was not sure which anymore. Not to Peggy back then in the ecstasy of first love. Not to Pamela now in the comfort of a good marriage. He lived at a masquerade ball, amid bitter music unending; saw himself standing near the wall, always smiling, never dancing. Except when he was in the air, the wind mussing his blue hair, his cape billowing behind him.

Then he was streamlined, whole, a perfect flying machine, a single entity, free of doubts, free of strife beyond the task at hand. At those times his heart was filled with the life-force, and he felt at one with his Creators.

Suddenly he heard voices. He had been drifting down toward the trees without realizing it. He checked his drift, and glanced down quickly. A car was parked in a lovers' lane. First he heard a man's voice, then a woman's, excited.

"Look, up in the sky!"

"It's a pterodactyl!"

"It's a dirigible!"

He got the hell out of there. Soared beyond a grove of trees, out of their sight. He treaded air, and turned on his superhearing. It still worked over short distances. He listened.

"I guess it was a pterodactyl."

"I guess. Kiss me."

He felt hurt. Eight years, and already they were comparing him with things extinct.

He climbed higher. It was getting more difficult now. His arms ached. His whole body ached. He was going to be sore in the morning.

He remembered the children. He started toward home. He searched out his house, and turned on his gamma vision. Like the superhearing, it still worked over short spaces.

The children were asleep in their beds, just as he had left them. But something was wrong. He peered closer. They had dark hair, not blonde. And they were boys.

The Levitan kids.

He realized his mistake. From the air most of Middleville looked alike. He had picked out the house set in the same position, but on the next block.

Mike and Sue Levitan lived there. One of his Top-Three couples. Mike, a lawyer, was out of town, handling a civil rights case in Tennessee. Sue was at the women's group with Pamela. Dolley Madison would be baby-sitting.

She was sixteen years old. Her real name was Dorothy Madison. Everyone called her Dolley. She was the head cheerleader at Middleville High. She got all the baby-sitting jobs she needed. Women liked her to baby-sit because they sensed she would be good in case of a fire. Men liked to pick her up and drive her home, because she had the prettiest face and the cutest ass in Middleville.

He switched his gaze to the family room, where Dolley would be doing her homework. She wasn't in the family room, she was in the living room. She wasn't doing her homework.

A gangly, pimply-faced boy was lying on the sofa. He was about fifteen years old. He didn't have any clothes on. Dolley was sitting, spread-kneed, on the lower part of his belly. She was gently rocking back and forth. She didn't have any clothes on, either.

He tried to avert his gaze. But his gamma vision seemed locked in place. From disuse, he decided. He saw Dolley Madison rock back and forth eight, ten, twenty times. Still his eyes wouldn't move, try as he might to move them. He saw her shift her position, slide her ass up the young man's chest, till she was squatting over his face, leaning backward, her hands gripping the sofa, her head thrown back, her eyes closed, her mouth open, her young breasts rose-tipped and reaching for the ceiling. As Mickey Spillane would have said, she was a natural blonde.

Thwack!

A huge wooden fist slammed into the side of his head. His vision went dark. Stars, question marks, exclamation points danced in his brain. He felt himself falling, falling; and landed heavily on the curb. He lay motionless for almost a minute, till his head stopped buzzing. Then he opened his eyes, and looked up.

A tall, thick telephone pole was towering above him.

He rested, sitting on the curb, rubbing the side of his jaw. He felt as if he had a hangover after some wild party; though he never in his life had been to a wild party. Then he stood. He was glad he had been drifting. If he had been flying faster the pole might have cracked, and the wires come tearing down. Half of Middleville would have lost phone service.

He was only a block from home. He walked the rest of the

way. No one saw him. There had not been a single mugging or assault in the entire history of Middleville. Still, no one walked in the streets, day or night. Going for a walk was something that grandfathers used to do, long ago.

Two hundred miles away, in Chevy Chase, Maryland, a late dinner was just ending at the home of Paul Vincent, the undersecretary of state for intercontinental affairs. His guest was Homer Bascomb, vice president of the United States.

It had been a social evening. Now, after coffee, the men carried snifters of Courvoisier toward the back porch.

"If Senator McGovern calls," Vincent said over his shoulder to his wife, "tell him I'm out for the evening."

He closed the French doors behind them. The two men stood by the railing in the dark, looking out over a rolling lawn that sloped to a flower bed. A large elm tree towered beside them. Children's swings were visible off to one side.

For several minutes they stared into the distance, neither man speaking. The vice president was clearly nervous. Vincent was not going to ease his discomfit by starting the conversation.

Finally the vice president spoke. There was a catch in his voice. He had to clear his throat, and start again.

"How's it going?" he said.

The undersecretary turned to him, his face a blank sheet of innocence. He sucked at his dead pipe.

"How's what going?"

"That's right, Vincent, the undersecretary said to himself.

Be mean. Be vicious. Play the cobra. But this poor slob of a vice president is hardly a mongoose. He's pure chicken.

He was partially repentant.

"Oh," he said. "You mean . . . the Project."

"What else would I mean?" the vice president said. "I mean the Indigo thing."

"Shhhhh!" Vincent hissed.

He turned quickly, and glanced at the French doors. The wives were still at the table at the far end of the room. He turned back, and walked slowly down the wooden steps that led from the porch onto the lawn. The vice president followed. They walked in silence until they were standing in the middle of the grass. The undersecretary looked up at the stars visible in clear patches between the clouds. He continued staring; playing games again. He didn't like the vice president at all.

Finally he said, "It started tonight."

"I know it started tonight," the vice president said. He was beginning to get annoyed. "How did it go? Has he shown up yet?"

"Indigo?"

"Of course Indigo."

"I don't think so. It's too early."

The men sipped their brandy in unison.

"What happens if he never shows?" the vice president said. "All those casualties . . . for nothing."

Vincent saw that he had been right. Bascomb was afraid of blood.

"We'll increase the pressure until he shows," he said. "If it reaches a certain level and he still hasn't turned up, then we know he's dead."

"That's easy to say," the vice president said. "But will the Russians buy that? Without seeing a body?"

The man's a simp, Vincent thought. An absolute simp. He placed his hand on the vice president's arm.

"Homer," he said. "We don't operate in the dark. If I tell you the Russians will buy it, the Russians will buy it."

"How can you be so sure?" the vice president said. Then he checked himself, and felt foolish. "Oh," he said, weakly. "It's all been cleared in advance. The Russians know all about . . . Mood Indigo."

Vincent flicked on his cigarette lighter with his thumb, to rekindle his pipe. The light crawled eerily over his face.

"Ach, sooo," he said.

When the pipe was lit he walked to the children's swings, and sat on one. The vice president, who was as portly as Vincent was lean, had trouble squeezing into the other swing.

"And if he does show?" the vice president said. "What then?"

Vincent looked at him sharply.

"Haven't you been briefed on this?"

"Sure, I was briefed," the vice president said, amiably. "I get briefed on lots of things. I can't keep every detail of every briefing in my head. I'm a busy man, you know."

Oh, yes, how *is* your golf game, Vincent wanted to say. He didn't. The thought crossed his mind, however, that it would have been safer if the vice president had not been told anything.

"If he shows," he said, "one of two things can happen. Most likely, he will be ridiculed by the world. He will be revealed as a mere shadow of his former self. A helpless bumbler, who is no obstacle to . . . world peace."

"And if not?" the vice president said. "If he turns out to be as powerful as ever? Then there'll be hell to pay!"

"That's not likely," Vincent said. "The project has been . . . several years in the making. It has been carefully planned. It's true that we don't yet know where he is, or who he masquerades as. But we have good reason to believe that we know his condition. If we're wrong, where has he been these last few years?"

"If you're wrong, you better talk fast when he comes busting your door down. And mine. And . . ."

"No names," Vincent interrupted sharply. "You never know what little squirrel is carrying a microphone."

He puffed at his pipe, calmer again.

"To answer your question directly," he said. "If we're wrong . . . then appropriate action will be taken."

The vice president shook his head. He squeezed himself out of the child's swing, and stretched his legs. His buttocks had fallen asleep.

"I'm not sure I like it," he said. "Taking the lives of American citizens . . ."

"Indigo is no citizen," Vincent said. "In case you forget, he was not even born on this planet. He is the ultimate alien. Nowhere in the government is there a record of his having been naturalized, either."

"I'm not talking about him. I'm thinking of those people up in New York. Innocent people getting beaten, maybe killed."

Vincent stood. He softened his tone. Acting.

"Remember the objective," he said. "It is to ensure world peace. How many wars have we fought to ensure world peace? In Germany. In Japan. In Korea. In Vietnam. How many citizens have given up their lives?"

"That was different," Bascomb said. "Those were soldiers. That was war."

"Inside the uniform of almost every soldier," Vincent said, "there is a civilian crying to get out. Just think of this as an extension of war. That's precisely what it is, you know."

He was getting bored with teaching the first grade. He looked at his watch.

"We'd better get back upstairs," he said. "The wives will be wondering."

When the vice president had left, Vincent closed the door to his study. He pressed the scrambler button on his phone, and dialed a number in Langley, Virginia. The ringing phone was answered by Martin Van Buren, deputy director of operations of the Central Intelligence Agency.

Unknown to the vice president, Undersecretary of State Paul Vincent was a top-level agent of the CIA. That fact was also unknown to the president, who had appointed him undersecretary of state; and to his wife, the former Candice Bergen.

"I just had dinner with Bubblehead," Vincent said. "He's a nervous wreck."

"I wish you wouldn't call him Bubblehead," Martin Van Buren said. "He might be president some day."

"Nevertheless . . ."

"Forget it. Bubblehead is not our problem."

"I know," Vincent said. "But I still think we should have cleared this with the president. We could have arranged for deniability. The president at least has some guts, some backbone."

"Yes," Van Buren said. "He also has some principles."

Brinkley's head still ached as he neared the house. He decided to try one more experiment: to see if he could still move fast enough to become invisible. He bolted forward at superspeed toward the patio, scooped up the broken glass, and leaped up and into the bedroom through the broken window. The dog growled on the patio, and then sniffed, sensing a presence; but didn't bark. The dog hadn't seen him.

Satisified, he placed the glass in the wastebasket near his desk. He would get some cardboard to plug the window. Tomorrow they would call a glazier.

Then he remembered who he was; his own innate powers. He was out of the habit of relying on his own strength. He had to return to that way of thinking again.

He lifted the pieces of glass out of the basket. He would rub them so hard that they would get hot, and melt. Then he would repair the window.

"Creeping Cronkite!" he said, in pain; and looked down at his hand. A shard of glass had cut into it, drawing blood. It was the first time he had ever cut himself.

He sucked at the base of his thumb. More blood came, slower. He wiped it on the thigh of his uniform.

Carefully this time, he stood near the shattered window and began to rub the pieces of glass together. This time it worked.

The glass softened, melted. With his hands moving at almost invisible speed he formed the melting glass into a sheet, and smoothed it into a clear pane. Then he blew on it, to cool it quickly. The window was good as new.

Suddenly he felt very tired: from the crash out the window, the flying, the bout with the telephone pole. He slumped into the wing chair near his Exercycle, to rest.

Two minutes later, he heard a car in the driveway.

Pamela.

He stood, and turned out the bedroom light. He crossed the hall. He was halfway down the stairs when he remembered. He was wearing his tights.

He dashed back upstairs, grabbed his clothes off the bed, darted into the bathroom. He peeled off the uniform. It was wet with sweat. He put on the clothes he had been wearing, and looked for a place to hide the uniform; and stuffed it into the laundry hamper. Carefully, he folded a towel on top of it.

He scooped the box of photographs off the bed, and returned it to the top of the closet. Pamela was hanging up her coat when he walked nonchalantly down the stairs.

"Hi, hon," he said.

"Hi, Pook."

She had called him that ever since they could remember. A nonsense word adopted in the babyhood of love. It meant nothing. It meant everything.

He kissed her on the forehead.

"How was your game?" she said.

"My game? Oh. Terrific. Oakland won."

"They didn't make the points, did they?"

He smiled. "No, they didn't make the points." She had a way of knowing everything.

They had met nine years ago, at a Halloween party given by Pamela's roommate. Pamela had dressed as a sultry Cinderella, in a ball gown and silver slippers, with her blonde hair falling devilishly over one eye. He had come as D'Artagnan, with a sword at his hip. They had talked, and danced, and drunk a lot, and stood in a corner and kissed while the party swirled around them. Then, at midnight, she had broken away from him, and rushed down the hall to her bedroom. He thought it was a joke, and waited. When twenty minutes passed and she hadn't returned, he knocked on the bedroom door, and went in. She was lying on the bed, her face smothered in the pillow, sobbing. He sat on the bed beside her. At first she wouldn't talk. Then, through her tears, she explained. This always happened when she was having too good a time. She would break down and cry, out of guilt. It was because of her brother. He was six years younger. He had been the best athlete in Fairville High. Till one day, clowning with friends, he had raced toward a swimming pool and dived in. Only there wasn't any water in the pool. He had broken his back. He was paralyzed from the waist down. He would never walk again. And here she was, drinking, dancing. . . . He had stretched out on the bed beside her, holding her, comforting her. They had fallen asleep that way, fully clothed. When they awoke at dawn they both had tender sides, from sleeping on his sword. But there was also a tenderness between them. He had seen a part of her soul, before he had seen her body. That was a reversal of the modern way—and there was power in it.

He had not been disappointed when, after several weeks, he saw her body. They were married a year later. And they were best friends still, despite the children. Few marriages in Middleville could make that statement.

They walked through the dining room to the kitchen.

"My God, what happened?" Pamela half shrieked.

"Oh, shit. I forgot. I had a flood."

"A flood? How?"

"Don't worry, I'll clean it up. Here, sit down."

He pulled a kitchen chair out of the wet area and placed it near her. She eased herself into the chair. She was bigger than she had been with the first two. They expected a boy.

"I was doing the dishes, and Punch called. We had a long talk. The water ran over. When I hung up, I forgot."

"How could you forget an inch of water on the floor?"

"Will you stop getting excited? I had a lot to think about. I'm cleaning it up."

He took a mop from the closet, and began sponging up the water. Pamela breathed heavily in the chair, calming herself. Her temper had been getting short as D-Day neared. She felt so puffy, so bloated. One thing she knew for certain. This would be the last.

"I'm sorry," she said. "What did Punch want?"

"There's trouble in the city."

"I heard."

He leaned on the mop, and looked at her. The pregnancy had rounded the angular lines of her face.

"Lady Madonna," he said.

"What?"

"You." He put aside the mop, and touched her face with his fingers. He sat in a chair beside her, and wrapped her fingers in his.

He didn't know how to begin. Lying to Pamela always had been the worst. Deceiving the others was a game. Deceiving Pamela was a sin.

He spoke directly, choosing his words carefully, so it wouldn't be a lie.

"Hon, I want to go off the copy desk for a while. Get back into the streets. It may be a bigger story than anyone knows. That's what Punch thinks, anyway. I want to cover it."

"You want to, or Punch wants you to?"

He looked into her pale-blue eyes. He imagined that Edith had had eyes like that, on Cronk.

"I want to," he said.

"Do it, then."

"I'm worried, though. About you. It may mean long hours, nights."

She looked down at her hands. Even her fingers were puffy. The wedding band was tight. "Of course I'd rather you were here." She looked up again, into his face. "But this is important to you. My mother's coming to help with the kids. I'll have her come tomorrow. She can drive me . . . if you're not here.''

"You're sure?"

"I'm sure."

"It's important."

"I know," she said.

Sometimes he suspected that she knew the whole truth.

When they met, Pamela was working in the traffic department of a prestigious advertising agency, Zit, Acne & Zit. (Does your product lack ZAZ?) Not long after, the agency had acquired the Stone's Furniture account. Pamela had gotten an idea. She spent several evenings drawing sketches, and showed the best one to the copy chief. It depicted a house made entirely of glass. The house was furnished with the company's furniture. A young woman was lounging on the sofa, reading a magazine. On the lawn outside, dozens of people stood, pressing their faces against the glass walls, peering into every room. The copy block said:

PEOPLE WHO LIVE

IN GLASS HOUSES

ALWAYS OWN STONE'S

The company had loved it. They had placed the ad in national magazines. They had even erected a glass house in a parking lot in downtown Manhattan, and had a fashion model live in it for three months (with Chinese screens placed in strategic locations when necessary). Thousands of passersby crowded around to look into the house every day. It was the furniture company's most successful campaign.

Pamela had gotten a large bonus, and had been promoted to copywriter. A bright career lay ahead.

Then Allison had been born, and Jennifer. She had never gone back to work.

Brinkley finished mopping the floor, and did the dishes. He turned out the lights. They walked slowly upstairs together, to the bedroom, and began to undress.

"How was your meeting?" he said.

"The usual," Pamela replied. "Me and Sue sat there all night listening to the other two. God, how they can bitch. That Abby! And Ann Landers! You'd think nobody in the world had problems but them. It's supposed to be a women's group. They use it as group therapy. I don't need that anymore."

"You've been saying that for a month."

"I know. But I couldn't just quit. They'd want to know why. I'd have to tell the truth and insult them, or else make up some dumb excuse. It's over, though. I told them I won't be able to come for a while, with the baby due this week. Sue's gonna drop out, too, in a couple of weeks. She says Monday-night football will be more liberating than those two."

He started to say that he had seen Dolley Madison baby-sitting for Sue's kids. He checked himself in time.

Pamela was naked, pulling her pale-blue nightgown over her head. He kneeled beside her in his green and white pajamas, and pressed his lips to her large round belly. It was smooth as a giant grape. He pressed his ear to her navel, and listened.

"I think he's kicking," he said.

She looked down at his wavy blue hair.

"What do you expect," she said, "with fourth and twenty-one?"

He stood, laughing; and held her shoulders.

"I love you," he said.

She kissed his lips, lightly.

"Me too you."

He turned out the light. They lay under the covers side by side, fingers entwined. It was darker than usual. The streetlight outside was out.

"Oh," Pamela said. "I talked to my mother today. I forgot to tell you about the rumors she heard."

"What rumors?"

Pamela's maiden name was Pileggi. Her father, Frank, owned a construction firm. After the wedding, he had taken Brinkley aside. There was a lot of money to be made in construction and related industries, he said. He offered him a job. Brinkley had refused, politely. Newspapers were in his blood,

42

he said. The smell of the ink, the roar of the presses . . .

They had both been talking in code. Pileggi's business was mob-connected. Brinkley knew it. They had never gotten close after he turned down the job. Though he loved Pamela's mother dearly.

"Ma overheard Pop on the phone," Pamela said, "talking to one of his . . . cronies. There's word out on the streets that someone has put out the biggest contract in history. Two million dollars! You'll never guess who's supposed to get hit."

"Who?"

"Guess."

"I don't know. Who?"

"Come on. Guess."

"How should I know? Jimmy Hoffa."

"Very funny!"

"Marlon Brando."

"Be serious."

"Let's see. Nixon."

"Nope."

"Castro."

"Nope."

"Not the president!"

"Nope."

"I give up. Who?"

"You ready?"

"I'm ready."

He felt the blood drain from his face as she said it. He was glad the room was dark.

"That's crazy! Who would think they could kill him? Who would even want to? He hasn't been around in so long."

"That's the strange part," Pamela said. "There are four different rumors on the streets about who put out the contract."

He was perspiring. He disengaged his hand from hers, and rubbed it on the sheet.

"According to one story, it's a couple of punks who want to rub him out. Imagine!"

"That's absurd. How could they do it? Where would they

get money for a contract? And why? They'd have to be crazy."

"Who knows?" Pamela said. "The second story is that there's Texas oil money behind it."

"But why?"

"Wait, there's more. The third rumor is—get this—the CIA!"

He tried to laugh. "If the price of tomatoes goes up these days, they blame it on the CIA." His laugh sounded forced. "What's the fourth rumor?"

"You ready?"

"I'm ready."

"The Russians!"

"Thank God. I thought you were gonna say Georgia O'Keeffe."

"You don't believe a word I've said." She sounded miffed.

He took her hand again. "Of course I believe you. I believe your mother told you every one of those things."

"But you don't believe they're true."

"How can I believe they're true? One: He hasn't been seen in eight years, so he might be dead already. Two: The only thing that can hurt him is Cronkite, and everybody knows it. He's too smart to go anywhere near the stuff anymore. Three: I don't see how anyone you mentioned has a motive. He doesn't seem to be bothering any of them."

"I know. But the word Daddy picks up is usually good."

He remained silent. She was right about that. Still, this was absurd.

"Good night, hon," he said. "I'm sure someone that strong can take care of himself."

" 'Night, Pook," she said.

And yet, he thought . . . and yet, just an hour ago, he had dug out his uniform . . . had been thinking of going back into action against those muggers . . . of showing himself in public . . . for the first time in eight years. Could that be coincidence? Or could someone be trying to lure him into the open?

But who? Who would know he was not what he once was? Who *could* know?

44

It's the darndest thing I've ever seen. It's almost as if the whole thing was organized.

Pamela was asleep. He felt her even breathing. Breathing for two. The child due any day. How could he go off now? How could he risk . . . anything?

He lay awake for a long time in the dark; thinking back to the glories of his youth. His epic battles with Logar, the mad scientist; with Univac; with Pxyzsyzygy, the elf from the Fifth Dimension. With Hydrox, and Oreo. With creatures from Mars, and dinosaurs come back to life. The raging fires he had put out, the explosions he had smothered with his body. The thousands of crooks he had put behind bars. The tens of thousands of times (it seemed) that he had rescued Peggy. All in a day's work, back then. Scarcely working up a sweat. Never knowing the meaning of fear.

He remembered his first case. It was the first day he had gone to work at the newspaper. He had saved a man from the electric chair. The man had been falsely accused of murder. He had found the woman who was guilty. She was a dancer, at the Mafia Club.

He remembered with a start the name of her victim; the name of the man she killed. It was Jack Kennedy. You could look it up.

A coincidence . . . or a prophecy? Who could say? Strange forces were loose in the world. Intrigues, conspiracies, malevolent plots that decent men and women could hardly conceive of. They always had been. They always would be. Until the final bang.

One in particular had been the most monstrous of all. The time the prankster Pxyzsyzygy stole the sun. All life on Earth had been threatened—till Brinkley plucked Mercury and Venus from orbit, and rubbed them together so they glowed red hot, providing light and heat. Later he spoke the pixie's name at the proper spot, and made him return the sun. It had all been a lark, Pxyzsyzygy said. Something about hell freezing over.

Every person alive had been in Brinkley's debt, back then.

45

Now the outbreak of muggings, and talk of contracts . . .

He tried to think of other things. He remembered Peggy. The nights on her sofa, lying naked together. Her long fingers; her willing lips; her knowing tongue (one of his Top-Three).

He was getting an erection. At this rate he would never get to sleep. He threw the covers back, and swung his legs off the bed. He went to the bathroom, and took a Valium.

It was morning in Moscow. Even the sun was gray.

In a private room of the Hotel Karl Marx, Oscar von Werner, the fat American secretary of state, was having breakfast with Werner von Oskar, the fat Soviet foreign minister.

(After the Second World War, the two great powers had competed for military superiority using Bavarian brains: our German scientists against their German scientists. Now, in the itchy peace, the field of contention had shifted. Now it was our German diplomats against their German diplomats.)

"To world peace," Werner von Oskar, the Russian, said, lifting his glass.

"To world peace," the Russian interpreter said. He had no glass to lift.

"To world peace," Oscar von Werner, the American, said.

They drank to world peace. Each side knew that the other had bugged the room.

They set down their orange juice, and began to feast on the goodies that had been spread before them: caviar on blini, herring with black bread, scrambled eggs with bacon, French toast, pots of steaming coffee.

"Seriously," the secretary of state said, "the disarmament treaty is ready. It has been approved by both our governments, down to the last semicolon. I am prepared to sign it this very afternoon. I think we should proceed."

"Seriously," the foreign minister said, "you know you are speaking—how do you say it—cow turd."

The Russian interpreter leaned over and whispered in the ear of the foreign minister.

"That is to say, bull shit," the foreign minister said.

The secretary of state wanted to reply immediately, but his mouth was stuffed with black bread and herring. He swallowed hard, and drank water.

"I mean what I say," he said. "We are prepared to sign."

"Of course you are prepared to sign," the Russian said. "We, too, are prepared to sign. As soon as the agreed-upon condition is met."

"And what condition is that?" the secretary said, stuffing his mouth with more black bread. It was the saving grace of all these trips to Moscow.

"You know quite well what condition," the Russian said. "We discussed it with Dr. Kissinger for years. And with yourself as well. You want me to speak directly into the microphone? That is fine with me. Publication of this condition will of course embarrass your government more than mine. We do not pretend, as you do, to a false morality. Morality is for the Danes."

The American realized that was true. The recording would be of little use.

"We are prepared to sign," the Russian continued, "as soon as we are convinced of *der Tod der Übermensch.*"

"The what?" the secretary said. His German was rusty.

The Russian nodded to his interpreter. The interpreter spoke.

"We are prepared to sign the treaty," he said, "as soon as we are convinced of the death of Overman."

The secretary of state giggled. The foreign minister grew pale. He leaned over and whispered angrily at the interpreter, *"Der Übermensch! Der Übermensch!"* He motioned for the interpreter to translate.

"The Overman! The Overman!"

The secretary of state could not stop his laughter. His mouth was full of bread and herring. His face grew red. He was choking on his food.

"Supe . . ." he said, and bits of chewed food sprayed across the table, into the caviar. "Supe . . ."

"Soup! Soup! Get him some soup!" the foreign minister cried.

The secretary, still red-faced and full-mouthed, shook his head. "No soup," he said. He managed to swallow the rest of his food, and drink more water.

"Supermensch!" he said, still laughing, and shaking his head. Tears were streaming down his red face.

"Supermensch?" the interpreter said, quizzically.

"Supermensch?" the minister asked. *"Vas ist das?"*

"Nein; nicht Supermensch," the secretary of state said, correcting himself. He wracked his brain. He always had trouble with names. *"Krankheit!"* he blurted. No, that wasn't it, either. *Krankheit* was German for sickness. What the devil was that code name?

The two Russians waited, amused.

"Ah! Indigo!" the secretary said, finally.

"Da! Indigo!"

There were smiles all around.

The secretary wiped his face with his handkerchief. His wave of laughter began again. *"Der Tod,"* he said, *"der* Indigo!"

The Russian shrugged. If it was humorous to the American, it certainly was humorous to him. He lifted his orange juice.

"Der Tod der Indigo," he said.

The American suddenly stopped laughing.

"Why are you so insistent that Indigo must die?" he said.

The Russian placed his fingers together in front of him.

"Indigo can catch our missiles," he said. "Indigo can fly here and destroy Moscow himself. We have no Indigo. You must have no Indigo. Otherwise there is no disarmament."

The American stood, abruptly. A steaming pot of coffee on the table tilted dangerously, but didn't spill.

"You will have your proof tomorrow," he said.

49

He wheeled, and stalked out of the room.

The Russian shook his head with a weary air.

"A Kissinger he's not," he said.

A few minutes later, the Russian minister and his interpreter were driving back toward the Kremlin. The minister made appropriate small talk. Then he twisted the rear-view mirror, temporarily disconnecting the microphone he knew the KGB had planted in his car.

"Overman!" he mimicked. *"Supermensch!"* He punched the interpreter lightly on the shoulder. "That was *wunderbar*, Yakov, *wunderbar*. That will give them a *gute* laugh in Dallas."

The Valium put him to sleep.
He dreamed of his parents; of his origins on the planet Cronk:

• • •

And God saw that the wickedness of man was great on Cronk.

And it repented the Lord that he had made man on Cronk.

And the Lord said: "I will destroy man whom I have created from the face of Cronk; both man, and beast, and the creeping thing, and the fowls of the air."

But Archie and Edith found grace in the eyes of the Lord.

And God said unto Archie: "The end of all flesh is come, for Cronk is filled with violence. Make thee a rocket of sturdy steel; a window thou shalt make in it, of durable plastic. Thou shalt place in the rocket thy newborn son, Rodney; and thou shalt fire the rocket to the Earth. For I shall destroy the planet Cronk with a fiery explosion; and all upon it shall perish; both man and beast, and the creeping thing. Only thy son Rodney shall survive, on Earth. And wear a weird emblem; and be a Savior."

And Archie heard, and trembled; and said: "Which Lord God am I speaking to?"

And the Lord God said: "This is the Lord God Nietzsche."

And Archie said: "Will ya lemme speak to Joe?"

And a low cloud burned with a bright light, and a deep

voice said: "This is the Lord God Namath. What do you want with me?"

And Archie trembled again in the presence of the Lords, and said: "The Lord God Nietzsche says he's going to destroy Cronk. Say it ain't so, Joe."

And the Lord God Namath said: "He ain't jivin' ya, kid. The big bang is at hand."

And Archie said: "Jeez!"

And Archie called his wife Edith and told her what they must do. And Edith said: "What are you, crazy?"

And Archie explained to the dingbat how the good Lords had spoken to him. And Edith said: "I think Bill Cosby has done this routine."

But Archie said that nonetheless it was true; that the Lord Gods planned to destroy both man and beast, and the creeping thing.

"Even the creeping thing?" Edith asked.

"Even the creeping thing," Archie said. "Not to mention the Meathead."

And Archie and Edith hugged each other, and wept. And Archie built a rocket of sturdy steel, and in it a window of durable plastic.

And the people of Cronk watched him, and laughed.

And Edith wrapped her newborn son Rodney in swaddling clothes, and swaddled him in the window.

And the people of Cronk watched her, and laughed. (They had never actually seen anyone swaddled before.)

And Archie and Edith fired the rocket toward the Earth; and hugged each other, and wept.

And the people who had come to the beach watched the rocket soar into the sky. And one of them shouted: "Go, baby, go!"

And the Lord Gods groaned, and destroyed the planet Cronk.

Nothing remained; not man, nor beast, nor the creeping thing. Only Cronkite, swirling in the Heavens.

And the rocket did fall to the Earth, in a place called Littletown. And it was found by an elderly couple, Franklin and Eleanor.

And Eleanor said: "Look, Franklin. A baby!"

And Franklin said: "The only thing he has to fear is fear itself."

And Eleanor gave Franklin a dirty look. And they took the child to a home for orphans. And in the home were building blocks, marked "A . . . B . . . C. . . ." And the child looked at the blocks and thought: "X . . . Y . . . Z. . . ."

And Franklin and Eleanor offered to adopt the child. And the director of the orphanage, Herbert Hoover, said: "Sign here."

And the Lord Gods Nietzsche and Namath winked at one another, and rested. For it was good.

● ● ●

Brinkley awakened, trembling. It had been years since he had dreamed his origin dream. The gray light of dawn framed the Venetian blinds. Pamela was asleep at his side.

He tried to interpret the dream. Was he like a drowning man? Was his entire life about to parade before him? And what was that new element in the dream, that XYZ? If ABC spelled the beginning . . . did XYZ spell the end? Was his end truly at hand?

He couldn't fall asleep again. He lay restless and itchy, watching the room slowly brighten; till Kojak's pet rooster crowed morning.

Brinkley dressed in the bathroom while Pamela was feeding the children breakfast. He pulled the uniform out of the hamper, and put it on. It was wrinkled in a thousand ways, like a waffle grown old, and it stank of perspiration. He winced in discomfort as he pulled his clean business suit and shirt over it. Like a newborn child, he thought, with the wrinkled, stale-smelling old person that it would become already encapsulated inside.

He realized how set in his ways he was. In the old days, when he was fighting every day for the triumph of good over evil, small discomforts such as a soiled uniform didn't bother him. Now they did. To most of his neighbors in Middleville, money was everything. To him, comfort was king. It was not a fact of which he was proud. It was a facet of his makeup he had come to accept.

If he had time, he decided, he would go down to the Lower East Side during the day, and see Max Givenchy, tailor to the heroes. He would get some spare uniforms made.

He hurried downstairs and kissed the children, and Pamela, who straightened his tie. He was feeling nervous, skittish, like a child on the first day of school. He drank his coffee standing up, and kept glancing into the family room, at the digital clock. It had been there for years, eliciting no emotional response. They had gotten it free when they opened a bank account. Now the passing minutes were like the tolling of bells. The exploding planets, like Prufrock's coffee spoons, were measuring out his life.

"Daddy, why are you going to work so early today?" Allison said. She was eating her toast and jelly cleanly, ladylike.

"Because I have extra work to do," he said.

Jennifer placed her toast jelly-side-down on the table. "Because Mommy is having a baby," she said. It was her answer to every question of the past few months.

He kneeled, and hugged them both. Their warm, smooth skin, taken for granted most mornings, was the world's most precious treasure.

"You're both going to be good and listen to your mother, aren't you?" he said. Both girls nodded. Jennifer, with idle intention, pushed her toast along the table as if it were a boat; leaving a sticky jelly wake.

He stood, and kissed Pamela, and told her he would call in the afternoon. She wished him luck. He took a raincoat from the hall closet, went outside into the gray, threatening morning, and squeezed his aching body into the battered black Volkswagen in the driveway. His arms ached, his legs ached, his thighs ached, his shoulders ached, from the unaccustomed flying. It felt good.

He drove to the railroad station, parked the car, and bought a newspaper. He caught the 8:56. It would get him to New York at ten.

The front page of the paper headlined the outbreak of assaults in the city. It was the early edition, it didn't tell him much he didn't already know. He put the paper aside, and glanced around the car, half-filled with the tail end of the commuter rush, almost all men. Some were reading the paper. Others had their eyes closed, trying to doze. Humanity being hauled from the sleep-warehouses of the suburbs to the work-sites of the city. And he was one of them.

He often told himself that he was different. He was not the stereotyped suburbanite made fun of in the *New Yorker*. He worked at the paper not just to make money, but because he was in love with newspapers. He had not sold his soul. And living in Middleville did not mean he had turned his back on the problems of the city—the poverty, the crime, the drugs, the ethnic tension. It was just that the air was cleaner out here; there was more room for the children to play, away from traffic. . . .

He studied the faces of the men around him. All of them, no doubt, believed they were different. Each had his own rationale. Each had his own secret identity.

He looked out the window. The window was cracked. Children liked to stand on suburban overpasses and throw rocks at the Swansdown Railroad. The cracked window created a pleasing effect. It took the symmetry of the suburban towns rushing by outside and fractured it into a dozen odd angles, tilting houses, chimneys, barbecues, swimming pools, TV antennas, picture windows, station wagons, into a violent earthquake, harmless, aesthetic. The middle class according to Braque.

He thought of a song from the Brel show:

> The middle class are just like pigs
> The older they get, the dumber they get
> The middle class are just like pigs
> The fatter they get, the less they regret.

Was it less they regretted? Or more? He wasn't sure of the words. At the moment he was overwhelmed by regret. Regret for the lost strength of his youth. The lost goals. The vanished confidence. He was alive and living in Middleville, after a fashion. But for how long?

A conductor in a gray uniform and gray peaked cap moved back and forth in the center aisle, punching holes in the commutation tickets of men who got on at each stop, glancing at a large watch strung across his vest on a gold-colored chain (on every wrist time was passing; even in vest pockets), calling out the stations.

"Nearville . . . Edgeville next!"

The idea wouldn't go away. It had been lying in wait for him when he woke up in the morning, like a playful puppy. He had thought it over, and decided against it. Now, in an instant, he reversed his decision. He decided there was nothing to lose; and perhaps everything to gain. He stood, quickly, and hurried down the aisle. He stepped off the train just before the doors closed at Edgeville.

Three taxi-limousines were parked at the station. He got into the first one. The driver, half dozing, awoke, and looked over his shoulder.

"Edgeville Sanitarium," he said.

The ride took ten minutes. The road wound through county parkland, the roadside elms and maples rich with autumn colors: browns, reds, golds. An argyle landscape under a straining sun.

His heartbeat quickened as they climbed a hill toward a stately brick mansion. The mansion had been the home of Elmer Fudd, heir to the Fudd Fudge fortune. After Fudd had put a rifle in his mouth and pulled the trigger, the mansion had been scrubbed down and donated to charity. Now it was a private asylum for the wealthy unbalanced.

He paid the driver, and the taxi pulled away. Dry leaves crunched under his feet as he moved through a wrought-iron gate and up a number of wide brick steps. His mind leaped with a thousand possibilities, each more horrifying than the last. It was a mistake to have come. He had no idea what condition the Captain was in. He might be an idiot, with drool on his chin. Or a strait-jacket case. Or catatonic.

There was no turning back. He needed the help, if there was any chance at all.

He tried the iron handle of a large oak door. It was not locked, which surprised him. He opened it, and stepped inside, into a large dim foyer. A nurse in a white uniform was seated behind a mahogany table, reading a magazine.

He approached the table; and was astounded. The nurse had blonde hair, a pretty, cheeky face, red lips, a full figure. She was a dead ringer for Marilyn Monroe.

"May I help you?" the nurse said.

Her voice was soft, almost a whisper; the thigh-soft voice of a sex child. Marilyn Monroe's voice.

He stared, incredulous. He looked at the black name-tag on her chest. It said Ms. Baker.

"Sir?"

He came out of his trance slowly, still staring at her. She smiled. Her teeth were dazzling. He blinked, and cleared his throat.

"I would like to see Mr. Button," he said.

"Mr. Button? Why, he hasn't had any visitors in years." Her voice was pure Karo syrup. He could have bathed in it forever. "But I'm afraid visitin' day is Sundy."

He bit his lip. "Couldn't you make an exception," he said, "seein' as how he hasn't had visitors in so long?" He had fallen into Ms. Baker's dialect.

She leaned forward. Her voice became even more of a whisper. "Well, the supervisor is home sick today," she said. "So I guess maybe it would be all right."

She stood, and wriggled, pulling her uniform smooth over her hips. He blinked. A dead ringer.

"Who shall I say is here?" she said.

He looked around. There was no one else in the hallway. He leaned close to her across the desk.

"Just tell him . . . a friend."

Ms. Baker peered at him, as if puzzled by his secretiveness. Then her face loosened, and she shrugged.

"You can wait out on our screened porch, through that door," she said. "I'll see if I can find him."

He watched the curves of her uniform recede down a corridor. Then he went through the door out onto the porch. It was bright with sunlight. Armchairs and lounges were covered with slipcovers in pink flowered patterns. Small tables with magazines on them were beside the chairs. Beyond the screen a manicured lawn stretched for about a hundred yards, and was surrounded by trees that almost hid the black iron fence. Two squirrels were playing on the lawn. He draped his raincoat over the back of a wing chair, and sat.

He half expected to hear screams from distant rooms. He didn't. All was silence. Perhaps, he thought, the wealthy insane were discreet. Or perhaps the Edgeville Sanitarium had sound-proofed its rooms. Or perhaps the patients were kept in constant stupors with drugs. Drugs injected into them secretly by Ms. Baker. Or perhaps there weren't any patients, they had all been murdered by Ms. Baker; and buried by her, out there, under the lawn. Geraldo Rivera ought to investigate.

The place was getting to him. Again he was sorry he had come. Perhaps he should slip out the door, now. Let her think she had imagined him. Just as he was certain he was imagining her. Marilyn Monroe, alive, and living in Edgeville. As a nurse. What a story!

He heard footsteps outside the door, and mice squeaking. The door opened. Ms. Baker backed into the room, and turned, slowly. She was pushing Billy Button, in a wheelchair. The wheels squeaked on the floor. He stood.

"My goodness, Mr. Button," Ms. Baker said. "As soon as your friend here leaves, I think we ought to oil your wheels."

She set him near the screen, where the sunlight could warm his face. "Now you two have a good talk," she said. "I'll be right out at the desk if you need me."

She turned and left, closing the door behind her. His eyes wanted to follow her; but didn't. He was staring at Billy Button. He looked perfectly sane; there was even a book face down on the gray blanket on his lap; it was *Fear of Flying*. But he had aged unbelievably. His hair was white, with shocks of wheat color. His face was parchment. His hands were gnarled veins and liver spots. He looked as if he were seventy years old. Button's hand, when he shook it, felt as light and dry and lifeless as one of the leaves outside.

Despite this—or perhaps because of it—he held the hand in his as they sat; a gesture of friendship, of warmth. He looked into the watery eyes beneath the lined lids.

"Captain Mantra," he said, quietly, respectfully.

A tic tugged at the corner of Button's mouth; a tic that was intended as a smile. For many seconds neither man spoke. It was as if they were acknowledging with their silence the solemnity of the occasion; as if they were waiting for invisible photographers to finish recording the scene for the history books; as if somewhere in the wings an unseen voice was murmuring a prayer.

Button gazed steadily into his eyes. When he spoke, his voice sounded old, but strong.

"At last we meet," he said.

A window was thrown open in a distant room of the sanitarium. Tin music drifted across the lawn, and curled onto the porch where the two men sat. The music was from a player piano. It was playing ragtime.

"I always hoped that one day we would meet," Brinkley said.

"Yes. So did I."

"But it never seemed necessary."

"Because we each could handle any problem alone."

"And there was no need to team up."

The tic that was Button's smile pulled at the corner of his lip.

"We sound like Hewey, Louie and Dewey," he said.

They were silent again; uncertain of what to say. Each was showing the other tremendous respect; regardless of their private thoughts.

"The arguments of millions of youngsters, eternally unanswered," he said. "Who was better: Mantle, or Mays. Who was stronger: you, or me."

Button blinked in acknowledgment. Brinkley studied his attire: the green sweater he was famous for, with the yellow band at the neck; over a white shirt and green tie. The sweater was tucked into his pants at the waist. It was faded, and beginning to unravel at the cuffs.

"You're surprised I look so old," Button said.

Years ago, Brinkley had meant to send a condolence card. He had let it slide, and then it had been too late. He regretted it now.

"I'm sorry about your sister," he said.

Button stared at his gnarled hands.

"You heard how it happened?"

He nodded. Button spoke anyway. Remembering.

"We were tied to the tracks; bound and gagged. We couldn't say . . . our word. The train was hurtling toward us. I wasn't afraid. We had been in similar spots a hundred times. I had faith that old . . . you-know-who . . . would save us. The train came closer. The track started to vibrate. An eighth of an inch, maybe, but it made the difference. I caught my gag on a spike. I ripped it off, and said the word. The lightning struck . . . and then the train. I bounced off, unhurt. I looked around for Mary. I didn't see her. Then, when the train passed, she was there. . . ."

His voice went dry, as if he had choked off a sob at that point a thousand times, in his memory.

"I didn't believe it. I looked up at the Heavens. I cursed them. I screamed. I shook my fist at them. As if I thought they would make her whole again. Bring her back to life. They didn't. I said the word. I became Billy again. I threatened them. I vowed I would never say it again unless they brought her back. They didn't. I wandered the countryside, shattered, for days, weeks. A hobo. A drifter. Out of my mind, probably. Then I went back, got all our money, and came here. Retreated from the world. I study. I read. And grow old quickly. Making up for lost time."

Button finished. There were unfallen tears in his eyes. His sorrow seemed as deep as if it had all happened yesterday.

"Still, if you wanted . . . to put it behind you . . . if you said your secret word . . . you could be Captain Mantra again."

"Yes. But I won't. Never again."

Brinkley took a deep breath, and exhaled. He wished he were somewhere else. Anywhere else. He didn't know if he could say it. The most difficult words of his life. He forced himself. For the children.

"Button," he said, "I need your help. I need Captain Mantra's help."

He explained what had happened. How for no apparent reason his powers had begun to fail. How he had retired, and married, and had children. About the muggings, the rumors of a contract on his life; about what unknown evils such a contract could portend for mankind. About how he had tested his powers the night before; how inept he was.

"Together, we could handle this easily," he concluded. "Alone . . . I don't know."

Button remained expressionless. He stared at the squirrels on the lawn. Then he turned back.

"Brinkley, you're a fool," he said.

"What?"

"You heard me. A fool. Getting yourself all worked up like this. And for what? Go back to your wife and kids. Forget the whole thing."

"Forget it?"

"Why not? You still want to be a hero? Throw some muggers in jail, win a warm place in the hearts of your countrymen? Bullshit! Grow up. Look at the world around you. There's no place for heroes anymore. Nobody wants them. They never did, not really. Think back. They always liked me better than you. And you know why? Because at least I was human part of the time, while you were always invincible. And what did they call me behind my back? The Big Green Fruit! I know it. And they liked Batman better than both of us—because he was all human. It's human weakness they cherish, not strength. Look what they do to their own heroes. The Kennedys. King. Yes, even Wallace, he was a hero to some. They shoot them down, that's what. You go back, make a fool of yourself, you think you'll get sympathy? The hell you will. They'll laugh. They love to see the mighty fallen."

Button paused for breath. The squirrels on the lawn were burying nuts against the coming winter. Brinkley was taken aback by the outburst. He didn't know what to say.

Button resumed, years of pent-up rage pouring out.

"You and me, we're dead," he said. "Over the hill. Comic book heroes. But it's not a comic book world anymore. Don't you see that? Our time has passed. Problems don't come in neat little boxes anymore, with 'The End' scrawled in the corner. There is no end. Only new versions of reality. People don't talk in balloons anymore. They curse. They shout obscenities. The world is no place for children; or heroes. Which may be the same thing."

Brinkley was finally beginning to react; to get angry.

"Why are you so bitter?" he asked. "Because of your sister?"

"Of course that started it," Button said. "But it's not just that. When I couldn't believe in the gods anymore, I tried to believe in humanity. But how can you? Look around. You wanna be a hero, punch out some two-bit crooks? What will that solve? Look at the real problems out there. Look at the smoking factories fouling up the air, the endless automobiles, the international cartels, the armaments, the poverty, the institutionalized corruption, the racism, the millions of babies starving. You gonna go out there and cut off all their peckers so they stop having babies? You gonna smash the factories that are pouring cancer into the rivers, into the food, into the lungs? You gonna round up every lying, cheating son-of-a-bitch in Congress, and in the Pentagon? First you figure out *how* to save them. Then come back and convince me they're worth saving. Then we can talk. In the meantime, I've borrowed one of their mottoes. Captain Mantra helps those who help themselves."

The ragtime piano tinkled in the background. Brinkley stood.

"I have to go now," he said.

"Do you? If you want, you could stay here. There're plenty of rooms. A home for retired heroes. No one would ever know. You've met Miss Baker? She takes care of all my needs. Every last one." He winked. "She's a regular marvel. No pun intended. What more does a man need?"

"I'm not sure," Brinkley said. "I'm not sure what, or why. But he needs something more."

He lifted the raincoat off the chair, and draped it over his arm. "Good-bye," he said; and he moved toward the door.

"So long, sucker," Button said.

Ms. Baker telephoned for a taxi. He caught the 11:20 out of Edgeville. The train was almost empty. Cracked windows refracted sunlight into diamonds.

He pondered the trials ahead. What should he tell Punch? What would he do that night if the muggers returned? Was it possible there was really a plot against *him?*

He thought of Button, sitting in his wheelchair. Possessed of the world's most powerful upper. And not willing to use it.

Button was wrong. Americans did cherish strength, probably to a fault. The home-run hitter lionized, the classy shortstop ignored. He, like Superman, had become an American symbol, an archetype, precisely because of his total strength. The cavalry charge. The Yanks are comin'. The B-52. America the Powerful. And if history revealed that the cavalry massacred women and children, and the B-52s bombed hospitals—if cynical men made a whore of morality—did that make it quaint to fight for what was truly good, truly just? Was morality dead, justice extinct, virtue an illusion: the province of infants and saints?

The diamond light was bothering his eyes. The thoughts were bothering his head. He was not a philosopher, he had never been introspective. He had always acted on impulse, responding to his perceptions of the moment. Relying on his instincts to do good; to know right. He preferred it that way.

Right was right, and always had been, and always would be. It was only when it conflicted with self-interest that it started getting complicated. There were not two sides to every question. Merely conflicting interests.

The diamonds disappeared. The train pulled in to the great dim cavern of Penn Station, an underground vault as big as a pyramid. He was glad to be rid of the thoughts, to stand, and leave the train, and ride the escalator up. On the second level he boarded the subway, and rode it one stop uptown, to Forty-second Street. From there it was a short walk to the newspaper.

As usual, Nelson Rockefeller was standing outside the building, in his tattered brown coat splattered with old wine stains, his white beard mangy, like a home for dirty birds, his shapeless gray pants torn at one knee and patched at the other, his feet wrapped in newspapers tied with string, his arm extended, calloused fingers poking through holes in green wool gloves, holding a tin cup. Some people said he was *the* Nelson Rockefeller, gone to ruin after the family fortune disappeared. Others said it was another Nelson Rockefeller, no relation. Nobody knew for sure.

Brinkley put a dime in the tin cup, for good luck. If he ever needed luck, today would be the day.

He entered the lobby of the building. Freddie News was at his stand, arranging magazines. The first edition of the afternoon *Post* was already sold out.

"Mornin', Mr. Brinkley," Freddie said. "Whadja think of last night?"

"You don't have to rub it in. They should've scored on that last play."

"Oh, the ballgame. Should I put another twenty on your tab? I was referrin' to the uproar in town here. Dirty spics and niggers!"

Freddie News was the most cheerfully bigoted person he had ever met. He usually steered clear of the subject.

"I was under the impression that at least half the muggers were white," he said.

68

"Who told you that, the papers?" Freddie said. "You can't believe everything you read in the papers."

Brinkley picked a pack of Dentyne from the candy rack, and let the subject drop. He put fifty cents in Freddie's black tray. Freddie gave him two cents' change.

"See you later," he said.

As he turned to go, there was a clatter behind the counter. Freddie's crutch, leaning against the back wall, had slipped to the floor. Freddie reached down and retrieved it.

Brinkley moved to the bank of elevators across the marble lobby, and waited. The lights indicated that all the elevators were on high floors. He saw the printers' elevator standing open at the far end of the lobby. He hurried to it, stepped in and pressed the button for the sixth floor.

The doors closed. The elevator began to rise, slowly. The printers' elevator was larger than the others, like a freight elevator. The printers used it to take carts bearing lead casts of the pages from the composing room down to the presses in the basement. The bowels of the newspaper.

The composing room and the city room were both on six. He got off, and walked through the composing room. It was a part of the paper that was in his blood. The smell of ink and oiled rags, the roaring clatter of the Linotype machines, inert lead bars melting into liquid, emerging as type, as words, stories, ideas, to be rushed in minutes throughout the city. The printers in their blue aprons and hats made of newspaper, setting the day's headlines by hand, snipping metal rules, securing the halftones, the photographs, in place. Mostly the smell, rushing through the system like wonderfully stale air, pungent with history. Television didn't have this, and he had missed it at NBC. Newspapers had a tail as long as all mankind. The presses, the written word. They traced back to the Middle Ages, to Gutenberg. And beyond, to monks with quills, in monasteries. And beyond that, to cavemen scrawling on stone walls. And forward again in time with a sense of freedom: the great satirists of England; John Peter Zenger; the First Amendment. All wrapped up in those sounds and smells that made his heart race. Radio, television, they had speed, but they didn't have history. He didn't deny that it was television, not newspapers, that molded public taste now. But he was not aware that public taste was any better for it. Now the paper was planning to spend millions to convert to a new system, a kind of photo-offset, that eliminated the lead, the Linotype machines; that involved only pasting up paper. It would save corporate money in the long run, they said. Brinkley wasn't looking forward to the change. There were certain traditions, he believed, that you couldn't put a price on. He was an etaion shrdlu man at heart.

He left the composing room, crossed the hallway, pushed through the swinging doors of the city room. Cluttered desks stretched for half a block. Most of them were empty, the reporters not at work yet, or out on assignment. Arthur Gold was not at his desk either. It must have been a late night.

He hung up his raincoat, and checked his box for messages. There were none. He moved across the room, toward the managing editor's office behind a wood and glass partition at the far end. Punch was at his desk, talking to a woman who was sitting on the leather sofa. He could see only the back of her head. He hesitated. Punch looked up, and waved him in. He closed the door behind him.

"Hi, Punch," he said.

The woman on the sofa shifted position.

"Don't I get a hello?" she said.

"Oh my God," he said. "Peggy! What are you doing here?"

She was wearing an orange wool suit and a white blouse. She was carrying a leather shoulder bag. A gray Samsonite suitcase was upright on the floor.

He sat beside her, and kissed her on the cheek. She squeezed his arm.

"I flew up for the big story," she said. "Nothing going on in Washington now can compare with this."

"Great," he said. "How long will you be here?"

A disturbing thought flitted through his mind: Pamela will not appreciate this.

"It depends," she said. "As long as the story lasts."

He turned toward Punch. "About the muggings," he said. "I'd like to go back on the streets for this one. If you can spare me from the desk."

"No problem," Punch said. "I want the whole staff on this one. Find out what the hell is really going on."

"As for the other," he said, "I haven't been able to locate him yet. I'll keep trying."

"You haven't?" Punch said. "Then who has? I guess he heard about it himself."

"What are you talking about?"

"Haven't you seen the *Post?*"

He shook his head. Punch reached for a newspaper on his desk, and shoved it across. He picked it up, and stared at the front page. He didn't believe his eyes. Great black letters across the top of the page said:

HE'S BACK!

A sub-headline beneath it said:

Battles Muggers in City

Beneath that was a large photograph of himself, flying at rooftop level, a scowling man dangling from his hand. The caption said:

Back in Action After Eight Years, Our Hero Carries a Suspect to City Jail This Morning. . . . . Story on Page 3.

His mind reeled. It was a fake, of course. An old picture of himself, retouched. But why would the *Post* do something like that? Knowingly spread a false story? He squinted at the picture. There was no sign of retouching.

"You feeling okay?" Peggy said. "You look pale."

He put the paper down. "No, I'm fine," he said.

The phone on the desk rang. Punch answered it.

"Yes, Scotty."

He covered the receiver with his hand. "I'll see you both later," he said.

They stood, and left the office. They walked together through the city room. As they had so many times before. For both of them, fond memories danced among the desks.

"It's been a long time," Peggy said. "How've you been?"

He thought he detected a shyness in her voice. That would be something new for Peggy. He was feeling a bit shy himself.

"Fine. Good. You look great."

She smiled, and brushed her hair back with her hand.

She did not look great. But her smile tugged at some left-over feeling in his chest.

He had loved her, once. In those days she had seemed a goddess. She was still an attractive woman, but now there were dark circles under her eyes; the beginning of crow's feet beside them; a few lines near her mouth. Time was doing its work.

He had not seen her since she moved to the Washington bureau. She had never married. He had heard rumors through the years, rumors that circulated about most women reporters at one time or another: that she would sleep with almost anyone to get a story. He chose not to believe it about Peggy. Especially when the rumors involved . . . the president.

"So, you're up here to cover the crime wave," he said.

She looked at him, sideways. "Crime wave? Are you kidding?"

"But I thought . . ."

"Him," she said, pointing to the picture in the paper. "That's *my* story. This time I'm gonna nail him. Find out where he's been for eight years. Find out his true identity, once and for all." She smiled her seductive smile (as opposed to her sardonic, ironic, and dumb-broad smiles). "Pulitzer prize, here I come."

He muffled a groan that erupted from deep in his belly; and turned it into a cough.

They passed near the city desk. He saw another copy of the

Post and picked it up. Recognition flared in his brain, lighting dark corners like a bulb in an attic.

"Goober!" he said.

"What?"

"Goober. That's Reuben Goober."

"What are you talking about?"

"This picture in the *Post*. I just realized who it is. I interviewed him a few times, years ago."

"You mean you know his secret identity?"

"Not him. The guy he's hauling by the collar."

He stared at the photograph. The question he had shoved out of his mind came reeling back; scratching a deep groove, like a cracked record; in the rhythm of an old joke: Who's that flying above the rooftops with Reuben Goober?

Stretch O'Toole walked quickly up the broad stone steps of the Cathedral of St. Mary. He looked about, to be sure no one was following him. In the vestibule, he crossed himself before the life-size wooden statue of Mary Tyler Moore. Then he pushed through the double doors into the cathedral proper.

Dim light filtered through stained-glass windows. Empty pews stretched darkly into the distance. The flames of candles lit by parishioners flickered in banks along the walls, beneath statues of the patron saints of the Church of America the Divine.

As his eyes adjusted to the light, he saw that no one was in the cathedral. He would have to wait. He moved slowly down the center aisle. At the main altar, he looked up at the marble works: St. Mary smiling down at him with her familiar half-smile; and clustered around her feet, her disciples: Lou, Ted, Murray, Georgette, Sue Ann. Two other figures were covered by white cloths. Stretch guessed that they were the heretics. Rhoda and Phyllis.

He felt serene here. He liked churches. You didn't have to think in churches. And if you did anything wrong, you were forgiven. It was like having a mommy again.

The only problem was the lighted candles. He had to be careful about those.

He was thinking of his dear dead Irish mother when he was startled by a cry from just inside the rear door of the cathedral. He turned, and saw a masked figure in blue leotards and a white cape leap into the air, and begin to fly around and around like a crazed bird inside the vaulted dome, around and around like an anguished soul trapped in the wrong body; till it jack-knifed, and straightened itself, and dove toward him blindingly out of the multicolored ceiling. He leaped behind a marble pillar. The figure landed easily beside him.

"You crazy bastard," Stretch said, barely able to speak over the flapping in his chest.

"Scared you for a minute, didn't I."

"Yeah, right. You think I'm stupid? I knew it was you all the time."

Slowly the newcomer peeled off a thick rubber mask that covered his head. It was Gimp. He held the mask out in front of him, like a headhunter home from battle.

"Not a bad job," Stretch said. "A little bit gruesome, holding it that way."

"It was terrific in the paper," Gimp said. "Did ya see it?"

"Yeah. The question is, did he see it. He must've."

"He must be dyin' somewhere, tryin' to figure out who it is." Gimp grinned. "You sure I didn't fool you for a minute? You looked mighty white there."

"You kiddin'?"

He wanted to strangle Gimp, for the scare he had given him. He was disturbed by his moment of terror. Was he really afraid of the coming battle? No, he decided. He had just been startled. When the time came, he would be ready.

A priest materialized from a side door. He glanced at them blankly, and kneeled briefly by the altar. Then he stood, and returned from where he had come. On the back of his black jacket, gleaming silver studs spelled out the words: IN GOD WE TRUST.

"Let's get down to business," Stretch said. "Here's the plan. We send the muggers out again tonight. He's bound to get curious. We leave him alone at first. See what he can do with them. If he can't handle them, if he looks foolish, then we keep out of sight. That's all we'll need. The whole world will see his weakness. That will be the end of it."

"And if not? If he polishes off the muggers?"

"Then I have a go at him," Stretch said.

"What about me? Why do you go first?"

"Because those are Peppy's orders."

"It's not fair."

"Life isn't fair. I go first. I should be able to handle him." He looked at Gimp. Gimp was smiling in a curious way. "What's the matter? You don't think I can do it?"

"I didn't say nothin'," Gimp said.

"Obviously, I can't fly," Stretch continued. "If he can still fly good, you'll have to go after him. But only then. Understand?"

"Yes, boss," Gimp said, with mock respect.

"Okay. Let's get out of here. Take off those leotards. And lay low till tonight."

They walked down the aisle. The front doors opened. Two ladies, one blonde, the other dark-haired, entered the church, chatting. Stretch and Gimp hid behind a pillar.

"But Miss Garbo," the blonde woman was saying. "Think of the money. A million dollars! Just to say that since you started using Per-Stop roll-on, you're never alone anymore."

The ladies passed, moving to the altar. Stretch shoved Gimp toward the side of the church. Gimp slipped through a small wooden door; and removed his tights in the confession box.

The thought of where he was made him slightly ill.

Brinkley sat at a vacant desk in the rear of the city room, staring at the front page of the *Post;* trying to solve the riddle of his second self. There were only a few people around who could fly; but there were many ways the photo could have been faked.

He turned to page three and read the story. It included a typical comment by the mayor, Alexander Portnoy: "I applaud his return. The city is in good hands."

Peggy was sitting at a desk nearby, making phone calls, trying to reserve a hotel room. She got one at the Albert Anastasia, a few blocks from the paper. It was in the heart of the midtown area, where the muggings had been the fiercest. A scared convention group had checked out: the Friends of Italian Opera.

"Newspersons rush in," Peggy said, to no one in particular.

She made another call; speaking softly into the headset. After a long pause, he heard her say, "Hello, Jim?"

He thought: Jim? Could it really be James Lowell Keith . . . the president of the United States?

It was absurd. There were two million guys named Jim.

Her voice was muffled, he heard no more. He was tempted to eavesdrop with his superhearing, but didn't. He turned back to the paper. She was holding the headset to her ear, tossing her head to keep her soft black hair out of the way. He couldn't

concentrate. Her familiar mannerisms . . . her familiar perfume
. . . brought back memories.

They had been hired by the paper the same week. They had
both become star reporters. They had covered the biggest stories
together, often sharing the same byline. By Dvaid Brinkyl and
Pegyg Poole.

But more and more often, in the midst of assignments, his
superpowers would be needed: to rescue a child from a burning
tenement; or repair a blackout; or save a sinking ocean liner; or
fight off a succession of monsters who waited in line like balloons in the Macy's parade to terrorize New York. (The Creature from Belle Harbor, he remembered. And Realtor! And Mad
Doctor Chancre. And O'Malley, the Rat Who Ate Brooklyn.)

When that happened, he would find some excuse to slip
away, into an alley or around a corner, and strip down to his
uniform, and put on his purple mask; and fly into action.

Peggy would cover the story alone. As often as not she
would get into big trouble—some brute or beast would snare her
(she had played Fay Wray to a thousand King Kongs)—and he
would have to dive in and rescue her. She would coo his
praises, her arms draped around his neck; and snicker about
that coward she worked with.

At least, she wasn't as dumb as Superman's chick, he used
to think. Superman didn't even wear a mask.

Increasingly, he became attracted to her. But he was afraid
to ask her for a date. He was twenty-two years old, and had
never been with a girl. Unless you counted Lorna Doone.

During Christmas week of the second year, the paper was
holding a dance. He spent four days screwing up his super-
courage. Then he said to Peggy, "Would you like to go?"

She said she would. She gave him the address of her
parents' house in Edgeville, where she would be staying.

He was terrified the next night as he picked her up. Tearing Hydrox apart with his bare hands had been easier.

Her father let him into the house. Her father was MacGregor
Poole, the songwriter. He had made a fortune writing hit

records, and scoring movies. His latest hit, "Let's Fuck," was still at the top of the charts.

He was staring at a snapshot in the living room—it looked like Jesus and Bobby Darin—when Peggy appeared. She looked beautiful. Her hair was piled high on her head. A brown silk dress clung to her perfect figure. She smelled of fresh-cut roses.

The dance was at Le Cuckold. Most of the staff was there, with wives or husbands, drinking at an open bar; stuffing themselves at a large buffet; ogling white-suited young Truman Capote, who had wandered in by mistake on his way to La Côte Basque; dancing to the music of Vanilla Douche.

When they were through eating, he and Peggy danced, close. His chest tingled with pleasure. Beneath the brown silk covering her breasts, there seemed to be nothing but Peggy.

He had never realized that she was so . . . three-dimensional.

He asked her out again the next night. They went to the movies, to see a documentary. *Invasion of the Body Snatchers.*

When they emerged from the theater, snow was falling. He drove back carefully. They parked at the bottom of a hill near her house; and sat in the dark, watching large snowflakes fall from a bright sky; watching the snow cling to the windshield and the windows; watching it build up thick, opaque; sealing them off from the world.

They kissed; and kissed again.

His hand was around her waist, inside her open coat. With his other hand, hesitantly, gently, he touched her cashmere breast. She did not protest.

His right hand moved under her sweater along her warm back. He reached her bra, and found the hook. He did not know if it would work, he was afraid he would break the mood. Or break the bra itself with his superstrength.

He pressed against the side, and pulled at the hook. The bra came loose. Silent joy spread through him. As if he had just defeated Logar on his home court.

He caressed her back, his other hand moving under her

sweater, up to her breast; pushing under the loosened bra; touching the warm skin; squeezing her warm breast, lightly; then harder, urged on by the mingled perfume of cashmere and flesh; finding the nipple growing hard against his palm; hearing Peggy breathing hard, moaning from far away. He was twisted in the seat, his pants suddenly too tight, kissing her, squeezing, and then he felt Peggy reaching for him, loosening his belt, felt her slipping her hand inside his pants—something no girl had done to him before—rubbing him hard through the cloth she thought was his underwear, seeking the hole in the fly. Not knowing it was his blue tights.

"Long underwear," he whispered hotly; and reached his hands inside his pants in the snow-soft dark, and struggled his uniform shorts down.

She found him, then, and began rubbing, stroking, playing with him, gently; both of them kissing, moaning. His mighty powers careened madly through his brain, twisted, distorted, ablaze. He was faster than a speeding mailman, more powerful than Mayor Daley, able to leap tall hydrants in a single bound. He realized that he had flown to distant planets to battle and destroy the enemies of men, he had swum the length of the ocean under water to repair a broken cable, he had snuffed out deadly volcanoes with his breath, he had subdued gorillas and angry dinosaurs, he had hurled blazing meteors back into space, he had forced the fissures of earthquakes closed with his bare hands, he had flown backward in history through the time warp, had talked with George Washington, Abraham Lincoln, Daniel Boone (they didn't have anything interesting to say), he had used his body as a drill and bored deep into the earth to put out smoldering fires in oil pools, he had welded railroad tracks together to stop trains from plunging off mountains, he had tilted the Earth back to its proper axis after it was knocked off center by a nuclear blast, he had flown into the blazing yellow depths of the sun itself to scatter sunspots—into the burning, life-giving center of the universe—all this before his twenty-second birthday, and all of it was nothing now, zero, zilch, boring, nothing compared with the helpless soaring ecstasy of this whispered moment, this teetering, plunging precipice of time suspended, when every man becomes a superman, the first time a Peggy Poole with knowing female fingers, all girl or woman, caresses, toys, plays with the pulsing ridges of his being, his hands on her hardened breasts, lips pressing, tongues commingling, toying, playing, stroking, holding; till twisting and shuddering in a dying fall he exploded wetly, softly, into space.

They held each other, for a long time. Then they straightened their clothing, and walked hand in hand up the snow-covered hill. He kissed her lightly on the lips, outside the door.

He drove home slowly. Halfway, he parked the car, and peeled off his clothing—the pants were wet anyway—and soared into the air in his uniform, just for the pristine joy of it. Higher and higher he climbed, looking down at the twinkling lights of the city, doing jumps and loops, spread-eagles, double-toe loops, wallies, sitzbends, salchows, double salchows, a triple-toe loop, a triple wally—even a Hamill camel.

The falling snow became Peggy's soft lips, kissing him all over.

When he woke up in the morning, he was in love.

Peggy was standing, putting on her coat.

"I've got a room at the AA," she said. "I'm going there to freshen up. I don't think he'll show till the muggers do tonight."

"Probably not," Brinkley said. He stood. "I'll walk down with you. I think I'll go to the Tombs. See if my old buddy Reuben Goober knows what's going on."

She got her suitcase. He carried it to the elevator. He felt slightly faint as they rode down in silence. The elevator had been inspected by R. Farina the past four years.

The newsstand in the lobby was closed. A hand-written sign said Out to Lunch. The *u* in lunch looked a lot like a *y*. It was Freddie's idea of a joke.

They pushed through the glass doors into the noise of the city. Nelson Rockefeller was shaking his tin cup. Peggy hailed a cab, and slid in.

"How about dinner later?" Brinkley said.

"Good."

"I'll call you."

She waved as the cab pulled away from the curb, into traffic.

He dropped another dime into Rockefeller's cup. The old man stank of whiskey, of not bathing; but was beginning to loom large in Brinkley's mind, as a talisman, a totem; somehow tied in with his own fortunes. The strong are weak, Rockefeller is poor, he thought. The last shall be first. The meek shall inherit the earth. Perhaps the millennium is at hand. Perhaps Jesus is coming. Or Morris Feinstein.

Somebody.

He walked toward the subway. The street was crowded with secretaries and executives scurrying toward coffee shops and restaurants for lunch. In the daylight, in the bustling street, the people seemed unconcerned with the muggings of the night before. The only indication that anything was wrong were the broken store-front windows, most of them already boarded up; and the olive-brown army trucks parked discreetly on the side streets, filled with wooden barricades and small contingents of guardsmen waiting till night.

He moved down the steps to the subway, bought a token for two dollars—it had a picture of Ralph Nader on it—and pushed through the turnstile onto the ancient, dank-smelling platform. Unexplained exhilaration welled inside him. Here underground he felt much as he had the night before, in the air over Mac-Arthur Park. The excitement of returning to the chase, he thought.

The train shook and rattled its way into the station. He boarded the first car, and sat. His eyes roamed the cardboard advertisements above the windows. The one great art form of the twentieth century: creating ludicrous needs where there had been none.

One ad said, "Meet Miss Subways," above a picture of a young woman. She was twenty-two, beautiful, a light-skinned black. "Janet Tyson," the copy said. "An artist's model, Janet likes to play tennis, cook, ride horses and lick dick." He couldn't take his eyes from her face. Except for the complexion, she looked a lot like Peggy had looked, back then.

He closed his eyes, and gave himself to the rhythm of the train. To the still-sweet memory of first love.

They had gone out every Saturday night after their Christmas romance. Sometimes on Friday night as well. They would go to dinner, or to a movie, holding hands, and they would wind up on the sofa of her apartment on Seventy-third Street, kissing, petting, rubbing each other into ecstasy beneath twisted clothing. She was everything he used to dream about, masturbating in Littletown before the sweater-wearing models of his mother's Bernat knitting books.

One night, the fourth week, stumbling, laughing, into her apartment on the wings of Beaujolais, he knew that something would be different. He went into the bathroom, and peeled off his uniform. He stuffed it into the pockets of his jacket; and put his clothes on again. They sat on the sofa, and began to pet; and it *was* different. They undressed each other, for the first time.

Slowly, hardly believing he was doing it, he rolled her last bit of clothing, her panties, down over her soft hips. He gazed at her perfect black triangle. Peggy lay motionless, waiting, eyes closed.

He reached off the end of the sofa, and found his wallet. He fumbled thickly with the zipper that led to the secret compartment. What was inside the compartment had been there for years, making a telltale indentation in the leather; making him almost more afraid of someone's finding his wallet than of someone's finding his mask, or his tights.

It was a picture of Jane Russell in *The Outlaw.*

Beneath the picture was a Trojan. The world's mightiest hero. Until Superpill. Peggy recoiled in horror.

"We can't," she said. "All those boys and girls seeing us in the comics. What would they think?"

He put the Trojan away. They continued to give each other hand jobs.

One night as they were lying together, Peggy's fingers encircling his pulsing thickness like diamond rings, he heard a faint sound, a cry for help, in the distance. He turned up his superhearing. It was a woman's voice, screaming in terror.

His impulse was to find out what was happening; to rush to her defense. But how could he explain it to Peggy, if he leaped out of her tender grasp, grabbed his uniform, dove out the sixth-floor window?

What excuse could he use?

His mind raced frantically, but he could think of none as he lay naked on the sofa, Peggy stroking him more frenzied now, the woman still calling for help in a terrible, mewling voice.

He began to perspire. He had to do something. But there wasn't any way.

Then, mercifully, horribly, like a tortured cat, the screaming died.

"What's wrong?" Peggy said.

His mind, palpitating, returned to the sofa.

"Nothing. Why?"

He looked at her face. His eyes followed hers, down to her hand. To the limpness she was holding.

He almost needed his supersight to see it.

He felt himself turning red. He tried to force a laugh.

Peggy frowned, determination in her gray-green eyes. She resumed her rhythm: stroking, pulling. She leaned her head down and caressed him with her cheek, her hair tickling his belly. She let her firm-nippled breasts brush against him. She tickled his soft sac. She yanked at him. He strained, mightily. It was no use. Nothing happened. The woman's screams were marching through his head. He was limp as a dead fish, belly up on a beach of guilt.

"Too much wine," was all he could think of to say.

He read about the woman in the paper a few days later. She had been stabbed to death in a courtyard, in Queens. Thirty-nine witnesses had heard her screams, and had done nothing to help.

The paper had it wrong. It was forty.

For days after, he was tormented. It was the first time he had ignored a cry for help. He felt miserable. He cursed himself for being a coward; even a murderer. Knowing it wasn't true. Not knowing what he should have done.

Eventually he made a decision. There was one time when he could not be all things to all people: when he was sharing a woman's bed; when he was (hopefully) nestled in her thighs. When he was fucking.

At such moments he must be lost to the world. There was no other way.

The decision seemed rational, inescapable. But it did not assuage his guilt. It did not silence the dead woman's screams. Twenty years later, he could hear them still.

The train was screaming around a curve. He was sweating at the memory.

More people had gotten on. He recognized a well-dressed man sitting across from him. It was Holden Caulfield. The famous proctologist. The one all the socialites used.

Caulfield was picking his nose. He made out like he was only pinching it, but he was really getting the old thumb right in there.

Brinkley averted his eyes. He returned to thoughts of Peggy. He recalled how six months after the incident with the woman— six months of renewed games—he had tried again to make love to her; had rolled on top of her, to press his way in. Without it, he might as well be dating Lori Lee. The mermaid.

"Don't," Peggy said.

He pressed harder.

"No," she said, and began to writhe, pushing at his chest, tears pouring down her cheeks.

Reluctantly, he rolled off her. He knew his strength. He dared not force her.

He was one of the good guys.

They lay side by side, staring at the ceiling. Neither of them spoke. Peggy cried. After several minutes, he said, gently, "What's the real reason? Is there a problem?"

She shook her head, yes. And sniffled in her sobs.

"I . . . I'm waiting for someone."

"What do you mean?"

"There's only one person I can make love to. Someone else."

He felt his heart sinking into his belly.

"Who?"

"I can't tell you. You'll hate me. You'll laugh."

"Peggy, I love you. I might cry; but I surely won't laugh."

"It's not that I don't like you. It's just this block I have."

"What kind of block?"

"I'm saving myself . . . my love. . . ."

She couldn't finish. She twisted her head away, sobbing; and buried her face in the pillow.

"For who?"

Even as he said it, the awful truth exploded in his brain, like a scream in the fun house. Swung him like a monkey by the tail.

For HIM!

She was lying face down, her nose still pressed in the cushion. She punched the sofa with her fist, in despair. Her beautiful buttocks shook. Beautiful buttocks inviting his tongue. His everything.

He wanted to laugh. He wanted to laugh and cry at the same time. His mind raced, seeking ways to phrase his questions.

"You don't know what he's like," Peggy said. She had turned her head to the side, the words came pouring out now, like water over a dam. "When he rescues me, flying through the air in his arms, curled up on his chest . . . He's so virile, so masculine. . . . I don't mean you're not, but he's so strong, so fearless; he makes me feel so safe. . . ."

"Have you ever gone out with him? Have you ever made love with him?"

"No. He refuses. He always has some good excuse when I invite him over, some dying child he has to go save. The man has no feelings! He doesn't know how he's torturing me. I dream about him, every night."

"Even after being with me?"

"Even then," Peggy said. "I'm sorry if it hurts you. But I can't help it."

He remained silent for a time. He thought of his uniform, squeezed with superstrength into his jacket pocket. He hungered to see the look on her face as he sauntered to the closet, pulled out the uniform, put it on piece by piece in front of her, the red boots, the white cape, the purple mask . . . leaving off his tights, perhaps; hanging loose.

He could taste the exquisite joy of it. Would she faint? Would she fall to her knees in front of him?

Would she laugh?

He didn't dare.

"If he doesn't want you," he said, "isn't it silly to wait for him? To carry this torch?"

"It's not silly," she said, bitterly. "It's sick. It's neurotic. Don't you think I know that? I've been seeing a shrink about it for a year."

"What does he say?"

"Say! What do they all say? He says it's Oedipal. It's because of my father. As a little girl my father was the strong one in the family. My protector. My hero. Now he's a big success, he's never home, he's flying off to the coast all the time to score movies; shacking up with Hollywood starlets anytime he wants. Choosing them over me. The only way I can get even is to score even better. To make love to the mightiest of the heroes. The greatest stud in the world. I'd be screwing my father two ways. It's the only way I can top him, and get rid of this hangup. A neat little Freudian knot."

"How do you know he's the greatest . . . lover . . . in the world?"

"Are you kidding? With his strength? With his powers? He's got to be."

Brinkley nodded. And said nothing. Then, hesitantly, he asked, "You've never . . . ?"

"Only once," she said. "With Demoniac."

"Demoniac!"

"We were lying here together. He forced me. He wouldn't stop."

Demoniac! Scourge of Evil. The very name seared his brain like hot wires. Demoniac! Child of Incest! Black-hooded Prince of Darkness!

"Where the hell did you meet Demoniac?"

"At a party," Peggy said.

The train screeched to a halt with a sighing of brakes. He opened his eyes. It was the last stop, River Street. He stood and stepped off the train, and walked along the dim platform. A subway billboard advertised a new film, Woody Allen starring in *Valentino*.

Poor Peggy, he thought. Desperate for him in the depths of her soul. And there was no way.

Their talk had been the beginning of the end. They had stopped dating soon after. They had become just good friends.

He climbed the stairs from the subway, out into the daylight. Poor Peggy, hell, he thought. Poor him! He was the one who had been heartbroken. His first love, the girl of his dreams. He had carried the sight of her, the smell of her, the taste of her, for years afterward; his hunger reinforced every day at the office; reinforced even more each time he dove to her rescue, to carry her off from yet another brute or beast.

Till he met Pamela. . . . Till Peggy went to Washington, and he could put her out of his mind.

Across the street was a grimy gray building, with bars on every window. Terrible, piercing screams issued from deep inside.

It was City Hall.

He walked two long blocks east, to the jail.

The limousine glided along a two-lane blacktop road in a remote section of Spudville. It passed a yellow road sign marked Dead End, and continued for another two miles; till the road ended at a locked iron gate, beneath a wrought-iron sign that said:

WINTHROP SCHOOL FOR BOYS

The chauffeur, wearing a black uniform and cap, stepped out of the car, and unlocked the gate. He returned to the car, drove it through onto a gravel road, got out again and locked the gate behind. The limousine crunched over the gravel for another mile; till it rounded a bend and came to a stop before a three-story red brick building crawling with vines.

"Very preppy," the tall man said.

The chauffeur came around and opened the rear door of the limousine. The two men climbed out. The tall man was wearing a black British topcoat and a gray fedora. He was Martin Van Buren, deputy director of operations of the Central Intelligence Agency. The short man was wearing a green velvet suit and a matching bowler, which was perched jauntily on his head, and carried a gold-handled walking stick. He was known by many names. One of them was Peppy.

"Nice location, eh Control?" Peppy said.

"Crackerjack," Van Buren said.

Van Buren had gone to Oxford, periodically, the way some men go to whorehouses, and he loved all things British. In preparation for his intelligence work he had read all Ian Fleming's novels twice. He liked to think of himself as Control (he dared not be Bond himself, even in his fantasies), and to address those around him by their double-zero codes. Peppy knew this, and was humoring him. These government types had to be babied, no matter how high they rose.

"Hallo. What have we here?" Van Buren said, in his best British intonation.

He was looking at a stocky barrel of a man who was lumbering toward them from the building. The man was wearing a navy blue pea jacket and a matching woolen cap, and looked like a refugee from a sea-going freighter, if not a three-masted whaling ship. A thin white scar ran from his right eye to his chin.

"Hello, Blood," Peppy said.

"Welcome aboard, Mr. Winthrop." His voice was both hearty and deferential; a belching smokestack in drydock.

Peppy nodded. "Blood, this is . . . Control. We're going to show him around the thchool. This is Mr. Blood, our headmaster."

The two men shook hands.

"Pleased to meet you, 009," Van Buren said. He was not sure what to make of this Mr. Blood. He was certainly not 007.

Blood looked at him with a puzzled expression, and then shrugged, as if to say: to each his own madness. He had seen stranger things in his lifetime. There was that lady in Singapore. . . . He cleared his throat. He was carrying a manila envelope, and he offered it to Peppy. "The reports you wanted," he said.

"Later," Peppy said. He looked even smaller than usual beside the girth of Blood. "First we'll show Control around the grounds."

They climbed into the limousine, Peppy and Van Buren in the back, Blood up front beside the driver.

"Once around the campus, Joseph," Peppy said.

The gravel road curled behind the house, and ran directly at a thick stand of maples. Then it divided at a fork. A wooden sign stood at the fork in the road, with three words carved into it:

SOLITUDE—ANGUISH—VENGEANCE

"The school motto," Blood said.

The car followed the left-hand turn, past a wooded area, into a cleared section of isolated cabins, once white, now gray and peeling. Each cabin was at least fifty yards from the next. Underwear and blue jeans were draped over clotheslines outside several of them.

"It was built in the forties, as a camp for unwed mothers," Peppy said. "We bought it in thixty-one, for a thong."

Blood pointed his thick arm toward the cabins. "Hoboes' quarters," he said. "Prepares 'em for the future. A cot, a desk, sink, toilet, hot plate. Nothin' else. Dormitory living would be counterproductive, as they say."

"What about food?" Van Buren asked.

"We run a grocery, down the far end. They shop there, an' eat in their rooms. Becomes a habit, after a time."

"How about socializing? None at all?"

"Not in a shark's ass, if you'll pardon the language," Blood said. "The school motto is the bible. Solitude."

The car moved forward, past the cabins, past another wooded area thick and dark with underbrush, to a clearing. Not far from the car, Van Buren saw a dead squirrel. Its paws were in the air. An arrow protruded from its stomach.

"Exercise area," Blood said. "We have a pool, green with chlorine. Very municipal. Only one boy allowed at a time. A running track, parallel bars, punching bag. And archery, for relaxation."

Shots rang out in the distance. Then more shots, closer.

"The shooting ranges," Blood said. "One for pistol, one for rifle. Some of 'em are practicing now."

"Together?"

"The only time," Blood said. "When they're armed. Keeps 'em on their toes. And the competition improves their shooting."

A tall metal scaffolding towered above the distant trees in the direction of the shooting. Blood motioned toward it. It looked like a giant guillotine.

"A building simulator," he said. "The platform moves up and down. Anything from a third-floor window to a fifteen-story roof."

The chauffeur slowed the limousine. "Shall I drive out to the ranges?" he said.

His voice sounded familiar to Van Buren; but he couldn't place it.

"No, Joseph, thank you," Peppy said. "We can head back now."

The limousine continued on the circling road; and pulled up once more in front of the brick building. For a moment they sat in silence.

"Bloody devilish," Van Buren said. "Almost British! A school for loners!"

The chauffeur came around and opened the doors. The men climbed out. Peppy took the manila envelope from Blood.

"Joseph, please brew us coffee in the library," he said. "Control and I will join you both there shortly."

Blood and the chauffeur took two steps toward the front of the building. A shot rang out. Paint chipped off a two-foot-high iron Negro jockey on the lawn in front of them. Van Buren paled.

"The lads are horsing around again," Blood said. "Great bunch of boys."

They continued up the walk. Van Buren followed Peppy toward a small door at the side of the building. Peppy opened it with a gold key. An absurd idea, Van Buren was thinking. A school for loners. Very . . . unprofessional. The agency was well equipped to handle any liquidations that were necessary. Oh, they had botched the Castro thing, and the reins had tightened a bit since the Church-committee nonsense. But this . . .

this school . . . was absurd. Fantasy of a dustman too rich for his own good. Wasn't even Harvard or Yale. Ah well. Part of his job. To humor wealthy eccentrics.

They entered a small anteroom; then a larger office, furnished in dark wood and leather, bookshelves heavy with leather-bound books. Peppy placed the manila folder and his walking stick on an ornately carved mahogany desk. Chippendale, Van Buren noted with approval. The midget at least had taste in furniture. As for his green suit . . .

"Come," Peppy said. He moved toward another inner office. "I want you to meet our honor roll of alumni."

God Save the Queen, Van Buren thought. Dutifully he followed the small man into the inner room. It was dimly lit. He saw four marble busts standing side by side on wooden stands. He could not make out the features.

Peppy turned a switch. The dim lights grew brighter. There was nothing in the room except the four busts on their wooden stands. The floor, the walls, the ceiling, were white marble. A mausoleum. Van Buren stepped closer to the busts; then recoiled, as if slapped in the face.

He stared in fascination. He recognized three of the four faces, without reading the names on the brass plates below.

Lee Harvey Oswald.

Sirhan Sirhan.

Arthur Bremer.

"You're joking," he said. He felt his knees growing weak. "Hardly."

"They . . ." His throat was dry. "All of them? Here?"

"Of course," Peppy said.

"But . . . it's impossible . . . they weren't the type to get involved in conspiracies. They were . . ."

"Loners?"

Van Buren rubbed his face with his hands. He had prided himself, ever since he had entered the intelligence business during the war, on never being surprised.

He needed to sit down. There were no chairs in the room.

"There were investigations," he mumbled. "Backgrounds

97

checked completely. Oh, sure, we fuzzed some connections with the agency, with the FBI. But this? There was no link between any of them and the Winthrop School for Boys." His confidence was returning. These busts proved nothing. Anyone could have busts made.

"Come, come, Control," Peppy said. "It would hardly do for us to leave links, would it?"

"But how? How did you account for their time here?"

Peppy smiled. "The usual," he said. "Phony passports, back-dated. Little old ladies who run boarding houses, turning up rent receipts in the identical handwriting, back-dated. Counterfeit W-2 forms. A girlfriend here or there. Fake diaries. Any number of witnesses to place them elsewhere. Not too many, of course. That would never do. They were loners, after all." He smiled like an orange.

Van Buren had new respect for the little man. More than respect. Awe.

"The fourth fellow," he said. He waved weakly at the unfamiliar bust, and read the nameplate beneath it. "Carl Robert Holmes. Who's he?"

"Martin Luther King," Peppy said.

"But . . ."

"I know. James Earl Ray. A hired gun. Very thloppy, don't you think? Carl Holmes had been thet up in Atlanta for months. He was going to make the hit a week later. They beat him to it. A cheap conspiracy. But we honor Holmes nonetheless. He gave his life in the thervice. . . ."

"Gave his life?"

"We could hardly leave him around, could we?" He sighed. "It's a very dedicated life our graduates lead."

They moved back to the larger office. Van Buren sank into a chair. He felt limp, wet under the arms. Here he was, involved in a plot to change the world. Thinking he was a prime mover. And discovering that he knew very little of reality. Like the blind man and the elephant, he was holding only a leg. And even that was slipping from his grasp. I should have been a pimp, he thought. The way mother wanted.

Peppy removed a folder from the envelope on his desk. He began reading names aloud. "Malcolm James. Carroll Richard Coates. Anthony C de Baca. Richard Leroy Manning. John Henry Curtis."

"Who are they?" Van Buren said, without enthusiasm. His spirit was broken.

"The best of the current crop," Peppy said. His eyes twinkled like stars in the heavens. "One of them will be the next honor graduate. Make a mental note of the names, if you care to. If you have any doubts."

"You mean . . ."

"When Indigo is disposed of, the disarmament treaty will be concluded. Both countries will destroy their weapons. That is the intention of President Keith, correct? Idealistic fool. But no true American can thtand by and let that happen. Once more there will be a job for . . . a loner."

"And Homer Bascomb will become president," Van Buren said. He was very tired. He wondered idly how J. Edgar had continued on into his seventies.

"Dear old Bubblehead," Peppy said.

"And he won't disarm, of course."

"He will follow instructions. We will have weapons—nuclear, everything. And the Russians will not. Nothing will thand in our way, anywhere in the world. America once more will dominate the globe. We will impose democracy everywhere. . . ." Peppy seemed about to float in the air in his enthusiasm.

"Capitalism," Van Buren said, wearily.

"Democracy, capitalism, what difference what you call it?" Peppy said.

Van Buren stood. "All of this hinges on Indigo being nullified, or destroyed. That's still an open question."

"A mere trifle," Peppy said. "But necessary. He's messed up too many plans in the past. This time we must be rid of him."

They left the room and moved down a long dark corridor, to the library. It was empty.

"They must be in the right-wing library," Peppy said.

"The what?"

"We have two libraries. One is filled with leftist propaganda. Marx. Lenin. The other is fascist. *Mein Kampf.* Father Coughlin. Pupils use one or the other, but not both. We breed loners of both persuasions, of course; so we have a choice, depending on the target; and the public opinion of the moment."

Van Buren nodded, vaguely. It had a certain mad logic. They moved across the hall, and joined Headmaster Blood in the second library.

"After coffee, my driver will return you to the city," Peppy said. "I have work to do here."

Van Buren leaned close to him. "Your chauffeur, Joseph," he said. "He looks familiar. Don't I know him?"

Peppy shrugged. "An old baseball player. For the Yankees. Used to play thenter field, I believe."

The jail—closed for a time, then reopened—was called "The Tombs." Its name had been changed to "The Happy Tombs," as a bow to prison reform. But the old name stuck.

The lobby was divided by yellow bars that stretched from floor to ceiling. On the near side was a pink desk, with a matching guard behind it. A telephone booth stood against the wall.

Brinkley started toward the guard; then changed his mind, and went to the phone booth. Home away from home, he thought, mocking himself. He hadn't used one in years.

Except to make phone calls.

He dialed the operator—she sounded like Mary Hartman—and placed a call to Pamela. He had to call collect. He had given most of his change to Rockefeller.

"Hi, hon."

"Hi, Pook."

"How you doing?"

"Good. My mother's here already. Nervous as a priest."

"And you?"

"Madame Cool."

"Nothing stirring yet?"

"Not even a mouse."

"I wish I was there."

"I know. Don't worry, everything's okay. If it comes Mom'll drive me, and Sue'll take the kids."

He hesitated. "It looks like the story's gonna be tonight. I may have to stay in town."

"I figured you might. It's okay."

"You sure?"

Was he seeking her approval? To evade any guilt? What if she said no, she needed him?

"I'm sure. Where you calling from?"

"The Tombs. I gotta see someone. By the way, you know who's in town?" She would know tomorrow anyway. "Peggy."

He thought he detected an extra beat of silence on the other end. He wasn't sure.

"How is she?"

"Okay. She looks a little bit . . . older, I guess."

"Don't we all."

There was an edge to her voice. Or was it his own nerves?

"You upset?"

"Should I be?"

"Honey. I love you."

"I know."

He pursed his lips, and blew a squeaky kiss into the phone. "I'll call you later. I have to go now."

"Don't."

"Don't what?"

"Don't go yet."

"I wish I was home."

"Me too. Come now."

"I can't."

"I know."

A silence.

"Pook?"

"What?"

"Do you own a purple mask?"

Another silence. Gut-wrenching. A silence that rattled the phone booth.

"A what?"

"A mask. A purple mask. Mom was doing the laundry. She found it in the hamper."

He reached into his pocket. It was empty.

A purple mask? Sure, I own a purple mask. And tights. And shorts. And a cape. And a jersey, with an emblem on it. I'm a hero. I'm courage personified. I prowl the Earth doing good deeds. I patrol the cosmos for my fellow man. I am goodness, strength, idealism, brotherhood, humanity. You didn't know that, did you? Not even you: wife, lover, best friend, mother of my children, partner unto death. Not even you know that about me.

I used to be all those things.

I swear it.

"Oh, the mask. Some company was giving them away last week. A Halloween promotion. I took it for the kids."

"Who put it in the hamper?"

"I don't know. Maybe Jemima."

Jemima was their cleaning woman.

Another silence.

"Pook?"

"What?"

"Be careful tonight."

"I will."

Neither of them wanted to hang up. It was one of their little games. His feeling for Pamela had never been like being in love with Peggy, all wallies and salchows in the snow. It was less evanescent; but more durable, steadier. A love that would last the distance. A married love. Still, they had their young lovers' games. As many now as on their honeymoon.

(On their honeymoon they had flown to Puerto Rico. It had seemed a painful waste of money to him, paying the airline.)

They hung up, eventually.

He made another call. To the Albert Anastasia. He reserved a room for the night. The room next to Peggy's.

The desk clerk clicked off. Brinkley noticed a scrawl on the coin box: Betty Eats Veronica.

He was upset. He never left his mask at home in the old days.

He remembered when he had designed the uniform. Choosing the colors he wanted. Checking the official catalogue—*Jane's Fighting Heroes*—to be sure he wasn't duplicating someone else's design; some minor hero in another galaxy, perhaps. Poring over swatches at Max Givenchy's, to find just the right shades.

At first he had thought it would be simpler to use his street clothes. It hadn't worked out. They gave away his identity. Also, police tended to fire their pistols at men flying through the air in Brooks Brothers suits.

If they had had double-knits or leisure suits in those days, he might not have needed a uniform. But they didn't. So he turned to the traditional cape and tights. The Italian acrobat look.

He had chosen red for the shorts and boots—the blood red of courage. Blue for the tights and jersey—the cool blue of intellect, of reason. White for the cape—the white of purity, of integrity. (That had been a mistake. The cape got dirty too quickly in the New York air.) And white for his chest emblem; the emblem that had appeared to him—he had never told this to anyone—in a dream.

He had studied it all in a mirror, and had liked it. But something was missing. It was too all-American. Too red-white-and-blue. Too . . . military.

So he had added the purple mask. A blending of the other three colors. The deep purple of the unconscious. The purple of crepe, of death. The purple of forbidden chambers. The dark mask of intrigue.

It made him look sexier.

Now it was in the hamper, with the dirty underwear.

A sharp rap on the glass startled him. He stood, and opened the booth. Judge Crater was impatient to use the phone.

The jailhouse guard, Bill Buckley, was reading *Screw*. As Brinkley approached, he shoved it into a drawer, and picked up a copy of *Corrections* magazine.

Brinkley showed his press card, and asked to see Reuben Goober, the prisoner who had been flown in that morning. Buckley checked a roster in front of him; and circled a name with a pen.

"Kareem Malcolm Shabazz," he said. "Petty larceny. If any larceny may accurately be described as petty, speaking in the moral or ontological, as opposed to the strictly legal, sense."

Buckley looked like a toy soldier in his uniform, a shiny black holster at his waist. His eyebrows leaped up like geese taking flight.

"Shabazz is the only denizen of the underworld our illustrious once-and-future aviatory superstar—he of the rococo haberdashery—has managed to deposit in our humble domicile this day. Or any day in recent memory."

He smiled his ingratiating smile.

It had to be Goober. There was no mistaking the picture in the paper.

"Let me see Shabazz, then," Brinkley said.

Buckley pressed a buzzer on his desk. Another guard materialized, and led Brinkley up a staircase, down a long corridor, into a lilac room. Wire mesh divided the room in half. One side was a cage, the other was not. They looked identical.

"Wait here," the guard said.

Pale light filtered through mesh-covered windows high in the walls. Brinkley had been in jails many times, and they always shocked him. Even at the peak of his superpowers he had felt guilty about putting men in prison. It made them worse, not better. But what else could you do? Even he couldn't solve that one.

And that was with humans. What did you do with Green Slime? With The Blob? Or Pxyzsyzygy, who could turn himself into vapor?

It was a problem the man in the street rarely considered.

Brinkley had compassion for The Blob, and for Green Slime. Their wrongdoing could be traced in part to difficult childhoods. The Blob, overindulged by his Jewish mother; Green Slime, discriminated against because of his race. But not Pxyzsyzygy. The fractious elf had grown up with all the advantages of the lofty Fifth Dimension; and performed his mischief simply out of boredom. And there were no limits to his pranks. Once, back in 33 A.D., he had gone so far as to . . . but there was no point in rehashing THAT.

A door opened on the other side of the room. Reuben Goober walked in. A guard closed the door behind him, leaving them alone. Goober approached the mesh divider warily, and peered at him.

"Hello, Goober."

"The name is Shabazz."

It was Goober, all right. Dark-skinned, lean and lanky. He had a small goatee now, but otherwise he looked the same.

"Since when is it Shabazz?"

"It's been Shabazz since I was born. Three years ago. You dig?"

"Okay. Shabazz."

Shabazz turned a chair around and sat, straddling it, the back of the chair between his long legs.

"The man says you're a reporter."

106

Brinkley extended his hand, to shake. The mesh divider was in the way. He pulled his hand back, feeling foolish.

"You're that Wicker fella, aren't ya."

He introduced himself.

Shabazz cocked his head, and squinted. "You sure you ain't Wicker, from the *Times?* Wasn't you hangin' around up at Attica?"

He shook his head, and sat in a chair, facing Shabazz through the mesh. "We talked years ago," he said. "When you were leading the movement."

"Oh, yeah," Shabazz said, uncertainly. He smiled. "All you honky reporters look alike."

It had been in the midsixties. Reuben Goober was one of the three best-known militant black leaders in the country. Stokely, Huey and Reuben. Promising to lead blacks into a new world; to leave behind the Uncle Toms of the National Association for the Advancement of Chicken Pluckers, as Reuben said into many a microphone.

Goober's history was well known. He had stabbed his first playmate when he was seven, because the boy kept calling him Reuben Jujube. He was sent to a progressive reform school: the Uncle Remus Camp for Wayward Nigger-babies. When he got out he turned to petty larceny, stealing fried chicken from the Colonel and watermelon from every fruit store he passed. "A product of my up-bringing," he wailed mockingly every time they hauled him off to the clink. Then suddenly he was eighteen, and Uncle Sam wanted to send him to Vietnam. Reuben wouldn't go. He had a one-sentence definition for that particular war: "The black man killin' the yellow man for the white man."

He spent three years in prison instead, reading law books and writing fiery pieces for the Op-Ed page of the *Times.* When he got out he became East Coast leader of the Panthers. Throughout the mid- and late sixties hardly a day went by when he wasn't leading a demonstration of one sort or another, to integrate schools, to improve slum housing, to secure more jobs for minority groups. Then came the Nixon years, and "benign neglect.'' Goober had dropped out of sight; till he turned up at Attica during the uprising there. He was serving two-to-ten for overtime parking.

For half a decade he had been a hero to young blacks. Now he was a relic of another era. The flip side of Amos 'n' Andy.

"What you want with me?" Shabazz said.

"Information."

"Why should I give you information? I don't have to talk to you at all."

"You're right. You don't."

"You're damn straight I don't."

"You can just sit here and hope somebody bails you out."

"What kind of information you want?"

"I want to know why you were arrested."

"That's what I'd like to know."

"What were you doing?"

"Nothing. I was carryin' a box of groceries for the Muslims' breakfast program for the kids. The motha swoops out of the sky like some fuckin' eagle in drag, and knocks the groceries from my hand, and hauls me away."

"Who?"

"What you mean, who? Superhonk."

Brinkley tried not to grimace. "You're sure?"

"It wasn't Peter Pan. He had blue hair, kinda like yours, an' blue tights, an' a purple mask, and that weirdball emblem on his chest."

"You mean ethnic clothing? It could have been anyone."

Shabazz didn't smile. "You ain't payin' attention, brother. I said this turkey could fly!"

"Did he fly good?"

Shabazz squinted at him. "What you mean, fly good? How should I know? I ain't never flied before without no plane."

"Right," Brinkley said. "Of course."

"There weren't no stewardesses, if that's what you mean."

"Right," Brinkley said. "Let's . . ."

"Food wasn't bad, though."

"Food?"

108

A smile split Shabazz's face. "Just jivin'," he said.

Brinkley smiled. They were wasting time.

"He brought you straight here?"

"First he flies to the *Post* buildin', where there's photographers waitin' on the roof. Then he brings me here. Jive-ass motha. They double-crossed us. They said he wouldn't show till tonight."

"Wait a second. Who double-crossed you?"

"Don't know his name. Tall, skinny dude. Stretch somethin'."

"You're losing me," Brinkley said. "How about starting from the beginning. Slowly."

Shabazz closed his eyes and shook his head, as if impatient with an uncomprehending child; and opened his eyes again.

"Okay, man. But listen good. I ain't goin' through this twice. I'm a Muslim, dig? We don't make much headlines lately, but we still doin' good work. Free breakfast programs for the kids in the ghetto. Classes in the afternoon, teachin' 'em black pride, black ideals. It ain't easy, brother, believe me, all them kids sittin' home watching "Good Times," goin' aroun' shoutin' Dy-NO-Mite, like it was some password to power, wishin' someday they could have an apartment like the Jeffersons. Hell, we tried real Dy-NO-Mite in the sixties, and it didn't do no good, but at least we tried. These kids are sittin' on their little black butts.

"Anyway, I'm teachin' the class the other day an' I pick up on some jive-ass talk. There's somethin' weird goin' down. Some dude downtown is offerin' fifty bucks to anyone who goes out in the streets Monday night, muggin' and slappin' heads and kickin' butts. Fifty bucks on top of whatever they clear, and they can stick it to some skirts too if that's their kicks. These punks whisperin' about it and just droolin' over the prospect. That ain't the way to go no more, I tell 'em, but you can see their eyes is on the white ass they're gonna haul. There's gonna be a meetin' of all interested parties just after dark yesterday, in this empty warehouse at Pier Fifty-two. I figure this is weird, I'm gonna see what's goin' down. So I slip into the meeting with the rest of them. There must of been a thousand punks there, black, white, spic, everything. This dude who calls himself Stretch is standin' on a chair, tellin' 'em the situation, just like I told you. There ain't no fuzz on the streets, he says, as if they didn't know, so there's no risk at all. Fifty bucks and all the hell they can raise, pig free. And then he says, there'll be a hundred more for them that does it again tomorrow, because by then the National Guard pigs'll probably be out. But the Guard is just scared-shit farm boys with rifles, he said, and nothin' to worry about. Then he adds, kinda in a casual afterthought, that the second night superfly might come around and try and quiet things down. Sheeet. But they shouldn't worry, he says, he has secret information that flyboy is just a weakling now, maybe can't even fly too good, and there's no reason to be scared. Lyin' son-of-a-bitch! But just to show good faith, he says, anyone who stands up to superfly will get still another hundred when the night is over. Well, I figure it up in my head, and that's two hundred and fifty bucks he's offerin' these cats, makin' a quarter of a million all told at least. So I figure it's all a gag of some kind. Then he's finished and tells 'em to line up at the door, and he steps down and opens this trunk, and damned if it ain't filled with fresh new fifties. He gives one to each of 'em as they file out, promisin' there's plenty more where that come from. So I take a fifty, figurin' what the hell, I listened to his speech, didn't I, and then I take the subway home to Harlem. And sure enough I hear on the radio that all hell has busted loose downtown.''

He stopped suddenly, like a speeding driver braking for a dog.

''Sounds to me like a typical stockholders' meeting,'' Brinkley said.

Shabazz didn't laugh. Brinkley didn't know himself why he was making jokes. Perhaps to cover his growing unease. He didn't want any of this to be happening.

''What do you think it's all about?'' he said. ''Where's the money coming from?''

''Beats the hell out of me.''

"This guy Stretch. That's all you know about him? Was he alone there?"

"Yeah. 'Cept for some cripple leanin' against the wall."

Brinkley pondered a moment; then stood.

"You have a lawyer coming to bail you out?"

"F. Lee Bullshit. They wouldn't let me call nobody."

"They have to. It's the law."

"Talk to that big-teeth guard downstairs. He's the law in here."

Brinkley reached out to shake hands. Again the wire mesh was in the way.

"I'll try and get my paper to put up bail," he said.

He rapped on the door. The guard opened it, to let him out. Shabazz stood.

"So long, Wicker," he said.

Brinkley was hungry when he left the jail. He bought a chicken taco and a Coke from a cart near the curb. He recognized the peddler as Roy Mack, head of the defunct Ronaldburger chain. Mack had lost his shirt when Americans stopped eating hamburgers. A sign on the red and yellow umbrella above his taco cart said, "Over 37 Served."

He carried his snack across the street, and sat to eat on a stone bench in the graveyard of River Church. It was the oldest church in the city. From where he sat Brinkley could see the tombstone of Robert Moses, who bought Manhattan from the Indians for a handful of trinkets in 1956.

As he ate, he became fascinated with the graves, with the stone and marble markers, scrollwork and cherubim carved into them by the sure hand of fate. In the past he had not concerned himself with death. He had watched the burials of Eleanor and Franklin in the graveyard of the First National Church of Littletown, but that was to be expected. They were elderly. They were mortal. Two states he thought he would never visit. (Like Kansas and Nebraska.) In his youth his life had stretched before him like a magician's colored ribbon, infinite in length, endless in its possibilities. Thinking of his own death had been like thinking of the outer border of the universe. What filled the place beyond space? There had to be more space.

(He had always intended to fly out there one day, and see

for himself. It was one of those pleasure trips he kept putting off—until it was too late.)

Looking at the graves, he found himself succumbing to that uniquely human experience, the fear of dying. It could happen to him. Perhaps even tonight, or tomorrow.

At least, he thought, death is "in" this year. His passing would be very trendy.

Apprehension crawled over his skin. He envisioned himself in a coffin, the lid being screwed down tight, sealing in the darkness. He heard the first clumps of earth hitting the lid, like heavy rain. The sounds growing fainter. The burden of earth heavier. Would anyone know, even then, who he had really been?

He didn't like worms. He wanted to believe there was a Heaven, where all the good souls who ever lived dwelled on perfumed clouds, in robes of white; listening to silver music.

He didn't think it likely.

A line of poetry drifted through his head: "Had we but world enough, and time . . ." —Andrew Marvell.

An ancestor of the Captain, perhaps.

The sun broke through the overcast that perched over New York each morning like a gray hen over an egg. The November chill was warming quickly to Indian summer. He tried to analyze the plot; to think of a plan of action. Mercenary muggers. Pay now, rape later. An attempt, apparently, to lure him into the open. A second him to rouse his curiosity. But why? Would they really try to kill him?

He could find no answers.

He was perspiring in the sun; and feeling uncomfortable with his tight, soiled uniform under his suit. It was like wearing a wet bathing suit that had arms and legs.

He remembered his resolve of the morning: to buy some new uniforms. He looked at his Mickey Mouse watch. Four hours till dark. He was only a ten-minute walk from Max Givenchy, tailor to the heroes. If some crisis was truly at hand, he might as well be dressed for it.

He tossed the empty Coke bottle into a trash basket—he had never been able to litter—and began to walk across town. Beyond the jailhouse was Little Italy: four-story tenements over cheap Italian restaurants side by side with funeral parlors. (It was an efficient arrangement. Patrons who got shot in the restaurants had only to be carried next door.) He passed the place where Joey Gallo got his. And Tony Corelli. And Sammy "the Clam" Sammartino. A three-star establishment. The smell of garlic drifted from the restaurant, mingling with the accents of four old men playing *bocce* beside it. Soon he, too, must squeeze the universe into a ball to roll it toward some overwhelming question. The swan song of J. Alfred Hero?

Beyond Little Italy came Chinatown, block after block of formica restaurants, all of them served by the same underground kitchen. And then pickle barrels in the streets, outside appetizing stores smelling of fish and vinegar. The Lower East Side, landing ground for the Jewish immigrants who had swarmed into New York from eastern Europe at the turn of the century. The younger generations had moved uptown, or out to Swansdown Island, but many of the old people remained, running their small shops, sitting in front of six-story tenements in canvas chairs, discussing their gall-bladder operations, waiting for the children to call.

Here in this oldest section of the city, among the Jews, the Chinese, the Italians, a sprinkling of Poles, an increasing spread of Puerto Ricans, Brinkley felt invigorated; in touch with a sense of roots. Though he did not live among them, he had always felt a strong identity with immigrants. Perhaps because he was one himself. The only Cronker in America.

He recalled his childhood. It had not been easy, adjusting. He had been different from the other children in Littletown. His blue hair, for one thing. But not just that. His strength. Other babies played with rattles. He could squeeze his to powder. He could pick up his playpen with one hand. He could throw a football half a mile. He could outrun the Silver Chief that passed through town every afternoon.

One day his foster parents had taken him aside, to confront the fact openly. Their words had remained etched in his memory ever since. His athletic scholarship to life.

"This immense power of yours—you've got to hide it from people, or they'll be frightened of you," his father, Franklin, had said.

"But when the right time comes," his mother, Eleanor, had said, "you should use it to help humanity."

Thus had begun his double being. With his true powers, the powers of his genes, of his heritage, of the planet Cronk—the old country—he was himself. But as plain David Brinkley, soft-spoken newsman, he blended with his surroundings. It was the same thing the sons and daughters of these immigrants did when they left the Lower East Side and moved out to Swansdown Island, into the American mainstream. He had assimilated.

Beneath his civilian clothing, of course, he had always been powerful. Just as, behind the drawn drapes of Swansdown Island, the sons and daughters of the Lower East Side continued to eat their garlic, their pickled herring.

Then, ten years ago, the attacks of weakness had begun; sporadic at first, then more and more frequent. He had begun to feel he was no different from anyone else. Like an artist or writer whose talent suddenly deserts him. He could find no solution, except to give in. To stop clinging to his superidentity. To accept the life of a mortal man. To be David Brinkley, nothing more. No different from any of the billions of creatures who have walked the Earth since time began.

In short, to settle.

So it had been for eight years. Till last night. Till today.

He turned at a corner, looking for the tailor shop. It was the right street: Lazarus Lane.

He wondered idly if it were named after he of the Bible, or she of the Statue. Either seemed appropriate.

Halfway down the block, he heard an ominous rumbling; the noise of a muted crowd. And then a woman's near-hysterical screams: "My baby! Someone save my baby!"

He darted through a dark alley, toward the cries. The alley

opened into a rear courtyard formed by the rear walls of tenements. About a hundred people, elderly Jews, younger Puerto Ricans, were milling in the yard, all of them looking up. His eyes followed theirs. At the sixth-floor level—the top floor—a rusty fire escape had torn away from the building. It was hanging at an angle about eight feet from the wall; dangling over the courtyard. Sprawled on the swaying fire escape, screaming, was a child, dark-haired, about two years old.

"My baby! My baby!" a Puerto Rican woman was yelling.

Two men were in a window nearest the dangling fire escape, trying to reach the child. They couldn't get within five feet of him.

"Where are the firemen?" a woman cried in anguish.

Brinkley stood rooted to the spot, staring. He had to save the child. A simple rescue.

Something he hadn't done in years.

A hundred-foot flight, and then down. Surely he could manage that.

. . . And hear, after so many years, the cheers of the crowd. . . .

He dashed into the alley, stripped off his clothes, stuffed them in a doorway. He reached for his mask.

He didn't have it!

Could he risk being seen without his mask?

He hesitated. Could this be part of the plot?

Absurd! He was becoming paranoid.

"My baby!" the woman screamed again.

He would have to risk it. These people wouldn't recognize him. Not after eight years off the air; eight years on the copy desk.

He hurried back toward the courtyard.

"There he is!" a voice shouted.

Brinkley froze. He was still at the edge of the alley. How had they seen him?

A loud cheer filled the yard. Then a sudden, total silence.

He stepped into the yard.

No one was looking at him. All eyes were staring upward,

at the sixth-floor level, across the courtyard from the fire escape.

A clothesline hung across the yard, passing two feet from the dangling child. Someone was climbing out a window; was balancing on the clothesline; was going to try to use the clothesline as a tightrope, to walk across the air; to rescue the child.

Brinkley stared with the others, fascinated. The man was dressed in black. Baggy black pants, tight black jacket. He had a soiled white shirt, and a black top hat. And a black moustache. He was carrying a black wooden cane. He looked battered, comical, as he stepped onto the clothesline, swaying in big shoes, holding the cane out from his body to help keep his balance.

"Ya think the tramp can do it?" a boy whispered.

"Shhhh," someone said.

Silence hung over the crowd. The child had stopped screaming, too; was watching, mesmerized, as the funny man in black, swaying back and forth on the limp rope, edged toward him.

Cautiously, one step at a time, sliding his feet, the tramp moved over the courtyard, toward the child.

He'll kill himself! Brinkley thought. He'll kill himself and the child. I've got to save them.

But he didn't move. He didn't leap. Is it fair? he kept thinking. Perhaps that old tramp can do it! Is it fair to take away his moment of glory? His moment to be a hero? I know what it feels like to be a hero. The average man has so few chances.

Standing at the rear of the crowd, unnoticed, he watched. Inch by inch the dark figure moved against the bright sky, closer to the child. The crowd was holding its breath.

"Noooo!"

A shriek arose as the tramp started to fall. He threw his weight the other way. The clothesline quivered wildly. The tramp regained his balance. There was scattered applause. Then silence, as he edged a bit closer.

He was two feet from the fire escape. The child started screaming again, frightened now of his would-be rescuer. The tramp inched closer. He grabbed the fire escape, lightly, with one hand. He looked down, and tossed his cane toward the crowd. It tumbled as if in slow motion. Someone caught it.

With his free hand, he reached for the child. The fire escape creaked where it was still hinged at the third-floor level. Gasps erupted from some in the crowd. They moved back, in case the fire escape came crashing down.

Straining, the tramp lifted the child. He clutched him to his breast with one hand. He extended his other hand for balance. He began to edge back across the clothesline, suspended in space over the courtyard, six stories high. One step. Two steps. Three.

The child, twisting with fright, kicked him in the stomach. The clothesline quivered. The tramp shifted his weight.

And fell.

"Creeping Cronkite!" Brinkley said.

The crowd shrieked in unison; a piercing roar in the gray, closed-in yard. Brinkley was airborne before the shriek began.

Like a dazed bird, the tramp plunged toward death in the courtyard, clutching the child to his breast.

People screamed.

For three stories they fell.

At the third-floor level they were caught, gently, by a hovering figure in blue tights, red shorts, white cape.

Then he dropped them.

"Creeping Cron . . ." Brinkley said, and grabbed wildly. He caught the tramp by the back of his black jacket.

The jacket began to tear.

He pulled them in, tramp and child, tight, to his chest. And held them. Then, slowly, he dropped toward the ground.

The crowd, stunned into silence, parted to let him land. He set the tramp down. The mother of the baby rushed forward. The tramp handed her the child.

"My baby, my baby," she cried, and clutched it to her breast, rubbing its dark hair.

The spectators shed their shock. A cheer arose; and then excited buzzing as they discussed what had happened, in a babel of sound. They closed in around him.

"Three cheers for the tramp!" someone shouted.

Someone else yelled, "Three cheers . . ." And then paused. Another silence fell over the crowd.

Brinkley turned, to thank the tramp for his courage.

He wasn't there.

"Where'd that fellow go?" he said.

A ten-year-old boy was standing near him. He pointed. Brinkley saw the tramp disappearing into the alley, walking in a funny way, his feet splayed to the side. Twirling his cane.

"I wanted to talk to him," Brinkley said.

"He's shy," the boy said. "He can't talk."

A young girl pushed forward from the crowd.

"Hey, mister," she said to Brinkley. "Why are you dressed funny like that?"

"Don't be rude," an old man said. "It's a free country. A man can dress however he wants."

The boy punched the girl on the shoulder. "Stupid, don't you know who that is? That's Captain Video!"

"Not Captain Video," a teenager said, moving forward. "Captain Midnight!"

"It is not either," another· girl said. "He's Captain America."

It's the mask, Brinkley thought. With his purple mask, they would know him.

He turned to the mother holding her child. Both were crying quietly.

"What's his name?" Brinkley said.

"Hay-soos," the woman said.

"Jesus," the young girl explained.

Brinkley nodded. It figured.

"Hey mister, who are you?" the girl said.

Just then bells and sirens filled the air. The crowd turned as one toward the alley.

"It's the firemen!" someone yelled.

Like a river overflowing its banks the crowd suddenly bolted toward the alley, to see the firemen with their axes, and the shiny red truck outside. Only the woman with the baby remained.

Brinkley leaned over and kissed the baby on the forehead. The woman clutched his hand, and squeezed it.

"Thank you," she said. Her tears were flowing again.

He lifted the woman's hand, and touched it to his lips.

"Thank *you*," he said.

He smiled, and turned, and hurried to the alley. It was deserted. Quickly, he slipped into his clothes.

In the street, the crowd was pressed around the fire truck. The children were climbing on it. No one noticed a man in a plain blue business suit walk away.

Just *once*, he thought. If only *once* they would notice . . .

There was a new, joyous spring to his step. He was exultant from the rescue. High on happiness.

He had some calculations to make. In the old days he would have caught the tramp at the fifth-floor level. Today he would have been satisfied with the first floor. But he had caught him at the third. His powers seemed to ebb and flow with his location. Something to think about.

It would have to wait. The shop was on the next block, second from the corner. The large window badly in need of washing. An armless dressmaker's dummy visible behind it. Faded ochre lettering on the door: Max Givenchy—Tailor.

He peered through the grime-coated window. Max was inside, his head bent low over the pressing machine, his white hair lost in the rising steam. The vivid past clutched at Brinkley's chest.

He retreated to the corner, turned it, and slipped into the familiar alley. It was dark and narrow. The second door from the end, once painted brown, was peeling. The words on the door were visible now more as an absence of paint—an outline—than as the presence of real letters. Still, if you knew where to look, you could make it out. It said Heroes Entrance.

He pushed at the door. It swung open. It will never be locked as long as there is breath in my body, Max had said once (in his gelatinous accent, a blend of English, Yiddish, German, and half a dozen other eastern European dialects).

He stepped inside. The door opened directly into the changing room. Since Max Givenchy knew him as a hero—had to know him that way, to make the uniforms—he could not know him as Brinkley. It had been the same with Captain Marvel, with Batman, with all of them. No hero is a man to his tailor.

Empty wire hangers hung from nails in the wall. As if they had been waiting for him all these years. He hung up his civilian clothes. He hoped that Max would recognize him. Sometimes Max mistook him for Superman. And pronounced it Zuckerman.

He opened the other door, which led into the shop; and stepped majestically into view. The Man of I . . . I . . . He could barely think it. The man of iron. Lowercase.

Max didn't see him. His head was still bent over the pressing machine. Brinkley felt his own heart pounding, as if with stage fright.

Max shut off the hissing machine, and pulled out the pants he had been pressing. He was a tall, white-haired bear of a man, his face lined with age, his hair splaying in all directions, a thick white moustache fringing his lip. He was wearing loose-fitting gray pants badly in need of pressing, and a red and black flannel shirt. A gray sweatshirt poked through at the neck.

"Hello, Max," Brinkley said, quietly.

Max looked up, over rimless bifocals perched low on his nose. He stared at Brinkley, saying nothing. His lower lip began to quiver. He dropped the pants onto a counter.

They began to move toward each other. Suddenly Max lunged at him, and threw his arms around him, clutching him in a great, sloppy hug.

"Mein boy!" he said. He was trying to hug him and pound his back at the same time. "Mein boy!" He pushed him away at arms' length. "Let me look at chu." He hugged him again. "I never beliefed you vas det. I knew you vould come beck someday."

They pulled apart, holding each other by the elbows. Max

dropped his arms, and pulled a handkerchief from his pocket, and took off his bifocals, as if to wipe them. He was brushing tears away.

"It's good to see you again, Max," he said. "You look good."

"Yeh, for an olt man, I look good."

"How's the wife, the kids?"

"Ach. Ver you been keeping youself? The kits? The kits are fine. All married, livfing on the island." He looked at the ceiling. "Sadie? Sadie died fife years ago. May she rest in peace."

"I'm sorry," he said. It was the second time today he was regretting someone else's misfortune.

"Yeh, dot's life," Max said.

He moved to the counter to busy himself, straightening the pants he had dropped there.

"I'm glad you're still here. I thought maybe you'd retired by now."

"Retired? Me? For vut? You tink I should move to Miemi, play pinochle all day? I'd be det in a veek. Here I keep busy, I talk to people ven dey come into the shop. Vun day dey'll find mein head slumped on the pressink machine, and dey'll bury me mit Sadie. Den Max Givenchy vill be retired. Not before."

"I guess that makes sense," he said.

"Sense? Sure it makes sense. Besites. Ver vould you fellas go if I retired? Ver you gonna find another tailor? The shop vould close. They're all closink. Who vants to be a tailor today? The kits? Nobody! They vant to be doctors, lawyers. It's a dyink art. You know vut vould happen if I closed? You'd have to buy your Zuckerman suits at Korvette's. Ready to vear, from the reck. Seams split the minute you fly in the air. Poof."

He imagined racks and racks of capes and tights. Regulars, shorts, longs. Extra longs. Huskies. The fat man's shop. Floor after floor of hero suits. Mothers picking them out for their little boys. Wives with their husbands. Some suits with sequined capes, for evening wear. Or gays. The whole city filled with men wearing masks and tights. In the streets. On the buses. In the subways.

125

That would give the muggers pause!

"You're right," he said.

"Of course I'm right. It's the same mit chu. You retired, you disappeared—I'm not criticizing, don't get me wrong—I'm not prying into your personal business, it's your own affair—but ven you retired, who took your place? Anybody? Nobody. Who vants to be a Zuckerman today? Or a Betman? May he rest in peace. Nobody. Eferybody's lazy, eferybody vants it easy. Max vorks hard. Zuckerman vorks hard. That's not for the kits today. Even the vimmin. They vant new careers, new opportunities. So look vut happened mit dot pretty little shicksa. Vut vas her name? Mary sometink."

"Mary Mantra?"

"Yeh, dots the vun. A cute little number. She used to come into the shop all the time. Skirts had to be just the right length, the bosom snug. I'm not complaining—she vanted good vork, and she vas right. She did good vork herself. So vut happened? May she rest in peace. After she vas kilt by a train, did chu see anyvun take her place? Any of dose new vimmin out dere? So vut happens. Ve got close dot don't fit, ve got crime in the streets. Dis is the new vorlt ve're makink? I'll be bedder off, soon I'll go join my Sadie."

Brinkley took his arm, and squeezed it. "Not too soon, Max," he said.

"Yeah, vell, ve'll see. So. Vot can I do for you. I'm too olt to tell meinself this is a social call."

He flushed. "I . . . I do want some new uniforms."

"So? Don't be beshful. Don't listen to an olt man. You vant new uniforms, dot's good. You're going bek to vork again. You vant sometink different, sometink up to date? A nice plaid, a herringbone? Maybe a paisley?"

"I don't think so."

"Some bell bottoms, maybe?"

"Just the usual. Only with a pocket this time. And a pouch under here, under the cape. So I can carry my clothes with me. Not have to go back and get them from a phone booth. With bubblegum on them half the time. Can you do that?"

126

"Sure, vy not? A magician mit needle and tread, dot's vut chu used to call me, remember?"

"I remember."

Max moved him toward a full-length mirror. He took a measuring tape from around his neck, and measured Brinkley's arms, his chest across the emblem, his inseams, his waist. Writing nothing down. Remembering the figures in his head.

"The belly's a little bigger, no?" Max said. "The vife makes good spaghetti, I bet."

"The belly's a little bigger, yes."

Max stood, breathless from bending. "I knew the vun I sent chu yesterday vouldn't fit."

Brinkley's eyes were roaming the shop. Little seemed to have changed. The special bolts of red cloth, and blue, and white, and black, were still stacked on a table against the far wall. Some of them looked dusty. The more commonplace materials were closer at hand.

He looked back sharply at Max. "What did you say?"

"I told dot kit it vouldn't fit, it vas too small. He vouldn't listen."

"What kid? You told what kid?"

"The vun you sent yesterday, for the uniform."

His mind went racing, ricocheting among molecules of unconnected dots. Trying to draw the picture.

"Let me get this straight, Max. You made up a uniform for me, and someone picked it up yesterday?"

"Sure. You mean you didn't get it?"

"No."

"But chu did order it."

"No."

"I got a phone call lest veek. Some man. He set he vas callink for you. Ordering a new suit. He gafe me the size. I told him dots too small, you alvays vore bicker. He set no, dot's the size you vant. So I made it. I fickured, who else knows you get your suits here anyhow? It must be legit."

"He didn't leave a name?"

"Nein."

"This kid who picked it up. What did he look like?"

"A kit, vut can I tell you. I mean, not a child kit. A kit kit. A young man. Mit a bad leg. Mit a crutch."

"And he took it with him?"

"Nein. It vusn't finished yet. I told him it's too small. He set no, it vill be good. He needed it lest night. I set, come beck in two hours. He set he couldn't, could I deliver it. I fickure, for mein friend, I find one of the boyus in the neighborhood to deliver. And dots vut I did."

"Where, Max? Do you remember where it was delivered?"

Max reached for a spindle on the counter. Pink receipts were impaled on it.

"I don't neet to remember," he said. "I got it written down right here." He riffled through the slips, peering through the bottoms of his bifocals. "Here it is. Deliver to Stretch O'Toole, Mafia Clup."

"Stretch O'Toole," he repeated, slowly. The name had a familiar ring. He couldn't place it.

"Tell me sometink," Max said. He touched his arm. "I did sometink wrong? I got chu in trouble?"

"No, it's okay, Max."

"I'm sorry," Max said. "I'm getting olt. Sometimes I don't tink so quick no more."

He squeezed the old man's shoulder. "You did fine, Max. It might be a lucky break. Give me a clue I needed."

"You mean it?"

"Sure I mean it. Now I know who to look for."

Max bristled with pride. He straightened his drooping shoulders with an exaggerated motion.

"Maybe ve should team up," he said. "Zuckerman und Givenchy. Like Betman un' Drobbin."

"Sounds like a law firm," Brinkley said. He smiled. "I've got to go now, Max. When can you have those uniforms? This one I'm wearing is pretty grungy."

"Let me see. Tights, shirt, shorts, cape, the veird emblems. Normally I vould say a veek."

"How about tonight?"

Max laughed. "Six o'clock. But not sooner."

"Thanks, Max. Could your boy deliver it?"

"Sure. Just tell me vere."

He hesitated. He couldn't use his own name, or even the paper. "Here," he said. He wrote down Peggy's name, care of the Albert Anastasia.

"Vait a minute," Max said. "I chust tought of sometink. You vant to get out of dot smelly vun, I got sometink you can vere underneath. Till tonight."

"It's okay, Max. Don't bother."

"Vait a minute, vill you?" He went to a back room, and came out with a dusty box. He pulled off the lid, and pushed back tissue paper. "It vus nefer claimed," he said. "You can hef it. Same size as you."

"No, Max, I couldn't. I . . . ."

He stopped. A small beam of light was beginning to glow in his brain. Like the first faint star of the evening sky. He wasn't sure yet, it was just a glimmer. The glimmer of a plan.

"On the other hand, maybe I will take it," he said. "Just for a day or two. How much?"

"No charge. It's yours."

"Okay. But put in a bill for the uniforms. Understand?"

"Yeh, yeh. You go catch some crooks, und leaf mein business to me."

Max closed the box. Brinkley took it, and carried it with him to the changing room. He felt in some obscure way as if he had come home.

At the door, he turned. "Thanks, Max," he said, softly.

"Don't be a stranger," Max said.

Undersecretary of State Paul Vincent had a headache. It had begun in the morning, as a tightness behind his left eye. It had grown deeper and more painful as the day progressed, despite four aspirins he had swallowed at the water cooler down the hall.

His headache was his conscience. He was in a dirty but necessary business, and often through the years he had done things he would just as soon have left to others. He had a clear perspective on his own abilities. He preferred to handle subtle maneuvers himself.

But the muscles and blood vessels behind his left eye had evolved into a valve, a regulator. When a job was too dirty, when it conflicted too strongly with a basic decency that he felt was the real Paul Vincent, then the pain would come.

He would curse it at first; try to will it away. It would not leave. It would grow stronger, more painful; it would begin to tighten every muscle in his body. Until he gave in; until he took some overt action to restore the harmony between his circumstances and his natural inclinations. He would become stubborn, adamant, defy an order, circumvent another—whatever was necessary to restore the harmony; to put his conscience to rest. When that was done the headache would subside.

Later, looking back, he would bless the pain he had begun by cursing. It had saved him from many a disaster; had kept him in touch with his own essential nature; had earned him a reputation for total integrity.

Each time the headache came, he determined to fight it, to overcome it. To be ruled by reason, not emotion. Each time, he eventually had to give in.

So it was today. By late afternoon, his head inflamed with pain, he told his secretary that he was not feeling well. He left his office at the State Department—so preoccupied that he forgot his coat—and began to walk the streets of the capital, trying to clear his head.

He passed the White House, its columned portico looking like a southern plantation (Tara, perhaps), and the Washington Monument, giant stonework goosing the gray November sky; walked beside the reflecting pool, among stray tourists aiming Instamatics; came to rest wearily on the steps of the Lincoln Memorial, Honest Abe brooding silently behind him. There he sat, trying to untangle the strands that joined at the blazing knot in his head. Remembering.

He had moved up quickly through the ranks. From Yale to London. Uruguay. Berlin. Berlin had been his masterpiece. He had planted seeds there that were still bearing fruit. Then the call home. His formal leave-taking from the agency (a fake, of course), his entry into the public sphere; his movement up the State Department ladder. A young man to watch, *Esquire* had called him. Little did they know.

He had met Candice, they had married. The actress and the State Department professional. His connection with the agency by this time so subtle, so dormant, there was no need for even her to be told. Charlie was born. They bought the house in Chevy Chase. A normal life.

Then had come the approach. A plan, a super-secret operation. They needed his expertise. They needed him to run an agent. Slightly irregular. Perhaps the most sensitive operation in the agency's history.

He had thought it over, had sensed the headaches lying in wait. He had refused. That was not the life he wanted anymore.

They hadn't pressured him. He was surprised. He kept waiting. No pressure. That was the one mistake he had made. He had written it off to some newfound humanity; had decided they had found someone else to do the dirty work and so had left him alone.

A month later, the president had named him undersecretary. They hadn't even put him on the shitlist. He should have been suspicious. Instead, he had been flattered; had let his ego be massaged; had decided the offer had been from the president's men, testing his integrity. And by refusing, he had passed the test. The theory made sense. He had clung to it.

Candice had gotten pregnant again. Had given birth to Mortimer. After six weeks, they could tell something was wrong. His eyes didn't respond properly. His muscle control was off. They took him to the hospital. Tests were taken. Brain damage. More tests. An operation. Bills piling up. Mortimer talking in that funny way. They loved him; but he would be in and out of hospitals and institutions all his life. The bills mounting, Vincent in hock over his head, unable to borrow anymore; the bank about to foreclose on the house. All of it a secret, of course. But not from them.

They made the approach as he was leaving the hospital one day, after visiting Mortimer. Exquisite timing. They renewed the proposal, on a bench in the park. The same plan was waiting. All he had to do was run an agent. Only this time he didn't have to do it out of mere patriotism, they told him. This time there would be a payoff. They would take care of the bills. All of them. They would take care of Mortimer's medical bills for the rest of his life.

He asked for time to think. He agonized. The bills had made him desperate. And Mortimer's welfare was at stake. He could get the best doctors, the best treatment in the world. Maybe somewhere there was a doctor who could help.

It became easy to rationalize. One more agent. In the service of his country. It would not be the worst thing he had ever done.

He had gone back to them. He had agreed. He had taken it on. He had poked the dead coals of his Berlin operation. A fire had flared in Moscow.

For years it hadn't bothered him. It had always seemed so abstract, so far in the future. But now the future was at hand. Mood Indigo was under way. Violence, assassination, perhaps even world war lay in waiting. Time was running out.

And his head was killing him.

He wished he could find out one thing. He wished he could find out if they were responsible for Mortimer. If some doctor, some nurse, in their employ, had used an X-ray, or had squeezed the baby's head—had caused the damage on purpose. To set him up.

It was six years ago. He would never know.

He stood, and resumed walking. He didn't know what he would have done if the doctors had been able to help. But they hadn't. Not even the tree surgeon.

It wasn't enough. That's what his headache was screaming. He was selling his soul for the mortgage on his house. It wasn't enough.

He knew what he had to do.

A breeze came up off the Potomac, and hurried down the avenues. The day was growing cold, and dark. The smell of rain was in the air.

He stepped into a drugstore, and phoned Candice. She had finished in the darkroom, was preparing dinner. He told her he would be home early. He told her to take Charlie and Mortimer to a neighbor's. He needed to talk to her alone.

He hung up, and walked back to the State Department. He got the Audi from the garage. Shivering, coatless against the cold leather of the seats, he drove home to Chevy Chase. Amid the hum of outbound traffic, with his decision made, his headache began to recede.

He parked in the driveway, and got out. The wind was blowing fiercely now, chilling him through and through. He couldn't find his house keys, he had left them in his coat. He opened the storm door, and rang the chimes. Candice opened the door. She smiled her uneven smile; the smile that owned his heart. But in her eyes was deep concern. She was bracing herself for whatever he had to say.

He looked at his digital watch. His spy training. Note every detail.

It was 4:17 P.M., Eastern Standard Time, when Paul Vincent came in from outside.

Stretch O'Toole. As Brinkley
walked across town the name buzzed around his head like a
pesky fly; but wouldn't land.

He thought of Kojak. Kojak knew the history of every crook
in New York.

He stepped into a phone booth on a street corner, carrying
the box Max had given him, and fished awkwardly in his pocket
for a dime; wondering how he had ever changed clothes in one
of these things.

Also wondering why. The damned things were transparent.

He called information; and dialed the Kojak house in Middleville. The phone rang for a long time. He envisioned Gloria
Kojak in the midst of diapering the baby. Before that she probably had done three laundries, scrubbed the kitchen floor,
cleaned up the shit the rooster had left in the den, done the mar-
keting, ironed the sheets. She would be wearing an old house-
dress that smelled. The thirty pounds she had gained since the
marriage weighed flabbily upon her. She looked far different
from when she had been Gloria Steinem.

"Hello, Gloria? This is David Brinkley. Is Theo there?"

"He's working. He started a new job yesterday. Consultant
to a private security firm."

"Which one?"

"Dillinger Associates."

He asked about the baby. They chatted briefly. Then he hung up, and called Kojak's new office.

"XYZ," a woman's voice said.

"I beg your pardon?"

"XYZ Industries. May I help you?"

"I was calling Dillinger Associates. Lieutenant Kojak."

"One moment please."

An extension phone rang.

"Kojak."

"Hi. This is David Brinkley."

"Ah, yes. The dog lover."

"I need some information. Confidential."

"Have you tried hitting him on the nose with a rolled-up newspaper? Preferably that rag of yours."

"You through, Kojak? This is important. Can you meet me somewhere to talk?"

"Real serious, eh, baby? Tell you what. I'm through here at five. My niece, the artist, is having a show on Fifty-seventh Street. I promised her I'd come. Meet me at the gallery if you want."

"Which gallery?"

"Gristede's."

"I'll be there."

He hung up. Kojak could be a real prick sometimes.

He shuddered. A delayed response. "XYZ," the woman had said. As in his dream that morning. ABC . . . XYZ . . . What the hell did it mean?

What did anything mean?

In his youth he had wondered often about the meaning of his life. Why had he alone been spared from the planet Cronk? What was his true mission?

Superficially, the answer was easy. He had been put here to help people; to save lives. To protect humanity from the Univacs. The Oreos. From Pxyzsyzygy.

But it didn't make sense. He might save a dozen people each day, but a dozen more would be killed somewhere else. He couldn't prevent every car crash, every mine cave-in, every

138

shooting. So what did his efforts amount to? Was he nothing more than a cosmic roulette wheel?

And that was when he had his full powers. What was his purpose now? To write headlines, to correct grammar in newspaper stories that would be in the garbage the next day? Was that a reason for a life?

During his recent attacks of anxiety he had wondered if he was not a superhero at all, but a schizophrenic. Had his entire life been hallucination? A lie?

He was walking west. He turned uptown on Third Avenue. The Bowery. Smelly ragged men sleeping off drunks in doorways. Men who had once been men.

Like himself.

He paused near one of them. The Tramp; dressed all in black. There is God, he thought. One minute saving a child's life. The next minute sprawled in a drunken stupor, his back turned to humanity.

Like himself.

He walked on. At the corner, he hailed a cab, and got in.

"Where to?" Bella Abzug said.

"East Fifty-third. The Mafia Club."

She drove like a madwoman. He should have known better than to trust the It's a Good Day to Die Cab Co.

The entrance to the club was beneath a red, white and green awning. Posters under glass flanked the doorway. "Topless Dancing," they read. "Bermuda Triangle." Smiling through the letters was a dancer in pasties and a G-string.

The poster stirred his memory. Something about the face. A face from the distant past.

The name fell on him like a meteor. Lorna Doone! His high school sweetheart.

He felt slightly ill.

He stared at the poster, feeling ashamed. The wonders of silicone. The face was Lorna's, but the breasts weren't.

He knew for sure. Lorna's breasts during his high school years had led him to develop his gamma-eye vision. One of his Top-Three powers.

She had lived next door to him in Littletown, in a white clapboard house, behind a picket fence, across a pretty yard. Lorna's body had begun to flower just at the time his own had begun making seed. One night he saw her pull down her shade and begin to undress behind it. He opened his window and peered at the silhouette on the shade; straining; wishing he could see through. Suddenly something clicked silently in his head. With an invisible beam his eyes bored through the ochre shade. He could see into her bedroom. The bed, the dresser, the mirror. And Lorna standing before it, her firm young body naked. Rubbing the pink nipples of her pert little breasts. Rubbing her pubic hair.

He felt himself getting hard. The window crashed down onto his neck. He pulled back quickly, so no one would see him peeping.

Excited, he moved through the house, testing his new toy. If he tried, he could see through the walls. Through the roof. Through furniture. Through clothing. The only thing he couldn't see through was mirrors, which reflected his own image. He couldn't see through himself.

(Not back then.)

He sneaked back to the bedroom, and peeped at Lorna in the shower. And slipped on the throw-rug near his bed, landing· heavily on the floor.

It was the beginning of another discovery. When he used his gamma-eye vision for the wrong purpose—to examine girls or women beneath their clothing—he was always punished immediately: by bumping into a wall, or tripping over his own feet, or falling down a flight of stairs.

He spent the horny high school years that followed battling the temptation. Still, under his picture in the Littletown High yearbook—The Pimple—it said:

David Brinkley
Clumsiest Boy in the Class

He always referred to Lorna as his high school sweetheart. But they had dated only once. He had worshiped her from afar as she became president of the drama club, treasurer of the literary magazine, and Most Popular Girl in the Class.

He refused to believe the leering whispers about how she had earned that title. Though he himself had seen her getting felt up against the baseball backstop by her boyfriend, Biff Bam.

(Biff was the fullback for Littletown High. He had dated Lorna for three years. Brinkley hated him. For years afterward, every time Brinkley was punching a crook or monster, as his fists boomed forward and landed on the villain's jaw, he would find himself grunting Biff's name.)

He pulled open the glass door of the Mafia Club, and stepped inside. It was dark, and almost empty. A couple sat at a small table in the corner. A lone woman sat at the end of the bar. Brinkley perched near her, leaving a vacant stool between. He ordered a beer from the bartender. As his eyes adjusted to the dark, he glanced at the woman. It was the dancer in the poster. Bermuda Triangle. Lorna Doone.

"Hello, Lorna," he said.

The woman was staring into a half-empty glass. She reacted slowly, turning to look at him; and then looked back into her glass.

"You are Lorna Doone, aren't you?"

The woman slurred her words into the glass, as if it were a microphone.

"What's it to you?"

"Don't you recognize me?"

She looked at him, as if not really caring.

"You with Alexander's Band?"

"I'm David Brinkley," he said. "From Littletown."

She drew her head back, and squinted. She seemed to awaken out of a boozy trance. She slid her glass along the bar, and moved to the stool next to his.

"David Brinkley? No kidding?" She raised her glass, and clinked it against his. "Howdy, neighbor." She drank. "Still peeping at girls getting undressed?"

"I never . . ."

"I used to see you, glued to your window, watching my shadow on the shade. Don't blush. I liked it." She waved vacantly toward the darkened stage behind her. "Men are still watching me get undressed."

"I guess it pays well," he said; not knowing what else to say.

"Not as good as the movies."

"I remember. You wanted to be an actress. Have you made any movies?"

"A few," she said. "I use a different name."

"What name?"

"Linda Lovelace."

Son of a bitch, Brinkley thought. All through the picture he had experienced *déjà vu*. Without knowing why. Now the image came rushing back from his youth: Lorna Doone at half-time of the Littletown High football games, dressed in silver sequins; entertaining the crowd by swallowing her baton.

"I didn't see it," he said. "I heard you were very good." He sipped his beer, embarrassed.

"You still on the TV?" she said. "I don't see the news much."

"I work for a newspaper now. As a matter of fact, that's why I'm here. I'm looking for someone named Stretch O'Toole. You know him?"

Lorna's muscles tightened.

"What if I do?"

"Who is he?"

Lorna shrugged. "Just a guy who comes in here sometimes."

"Was he here last night?"

"You sure you're not a cop?"

"I swear."

She sipped her drink. "Maybe he was here."

"With someone else? A kid with a crutch?"

"Maybe. And another one. A fop. Real tiny."

"You know their names?"

She shook her head. "Why do you want Stretch?"

"He's trying . . ." to kill me, Brinkley started to say. He checked himself. "I just need to talk to him. You know where he lives?"

She shook her head again, without looking at him. He could tell she was lying.

"You're sure?"

"Yes."

"It's important. There could be lives at stake."

"What do you want from me?" she said, her temper flashing. "Leave me alone! Leave my life alone!"

The bartender moved toward them. "This guy bothering you?"

She calmed herself quickly. "It's okay," she said. She slid off the stool. "I've got to go now. Nice to see you, David." She crossed the small stage, and disappeared through a door behind it.

The stage reminded him of the night she had played Joan of Arc with the Littletown High Players. She had looked so pretty, her auburn hair falling over her white costume. Tears had clouded his eyes as she was tied to the stake, as the faggots were lighted. Her screams had sounded so real. Suddenly he had realized they were real. The flames were out of control. He had leaped from his seat, faster than the human eye could see. He flew to the stage, blew out the flames with his superbreath, untied the ropes that bound her. He was back in his seat before anyone noticed.

Her burns were minor. She never knew it, but he had saved her life. She was the first of the multitudes.

The bartender removed her empty glass.

"Tell me about Stretch O'Toole," Brinkley said.

"Bermuda's quite a girl," the bartender said. "Traveled all over the world. Groupie to the superheroes."

"Groupie?"

"You should hear the stories she tells. Makin' it with Superman while he's pumping so fast he's invisible. Batman and Robin, front and back. The Lone Ranger, while Tonto held her down. And Wonder Woman! Ask her about Wonder Woman."

143

"Funny that I never . . . heard of her," Brinkley said.

It's like a New Yorker who's never been to the top of the Empire State Building, he thought.

He wasn't sure if he meant her, or himself.

Without warning, music erupted from a three-piece combo that had slipped quietly onto the stage. A white spotlight beamed. Lorna Doone stepped into it, half naked; as into a milk bath. And began to dance.

Queen of the senior prom, Brinkley thought. He had been her escort. After Biff left town.

Their only date.

He paid for his beer. In the street, he flagged a cab, and slid in.

"Where to?" Bella Abzug said.

Kojak's niece, after painting without recognition for a dozen years, had suddenly been discovered. Critics were calling her the best American painter of the century. Her first New York exhibition was a major event of the fall social season.

As Brinkley moved through the champagne buzz of the gallery looking for Kojak, he recognized many faces, among them the Countess Felix Mantilla; the Duchess of Hoyt-Wilhelm; fashion designer Emil Verban; the much-publicized southern debutante Kirby Higby; millionaire philanthropist Goody Rosen; porn film queen Sandy Amoros and her leading man, Herb Score; the Most Rev. Luke Easter; pop artist Andy Pafko; jockey Eddie Gaedel; parapsychologist Ryne Duren; the recently remarried Bobo Holliman; the French ambassador, Claude Passeau; stripper Nellie Fox; Karl Spooner, the Jungian analyst; ballerina Tookie Gilbert; potato chip magnate Al Gionfriddo; evangelist Enos Slaughter; Gene Hermanski, the film director; Washington hostess Choo Choo Coleman; *Playboy*'s Playmate of the Year, Tracy Stallard; and others.

Standing demurely in one corner, accepting congratulations from well-wishers, amid the popping of flashbulbs, was the artist—a pretty, dark-haired young woman named Carol Mothner.

Kojak was not in sight. Brinkley took a glass of champagne

from a passing waiter. He moved from room to room, looking
at the works of art as best he could through the crowd; overhear-
ing random comments.

"The intuitive analysis of the geometric forms lends a lyri-
cal abstractionism to the atmospheric shapeliness," said the
Countess Felix Mantilla.

"The diagrammatic borderlines where the mandala ends and
the viscera begin reveal formal yet subjective parallels and con-
tinuities to historical projections, increasing the complexity of
both," said Jeff Heath, assistant to Mayor Portnoy.

"The interior form dominating with its dark hues the pure
white element riskily transcends the frantic atmosphere distilled
from the ritualized yet sophisticated intellectualization," said
Georgia heiress Peanuts Lowry.

"I was going to say," said Supreme Court Justice Charlie
Brown, "that it looks like a ducky and a horsey."

What they were looking at were translucent sculptures Ms.
Mothner had devised for her New York show: thin skins of
gaily colored rubber, inflated with air or helium, and tied with
string at a nipple. The sculptures hung from the ceiling, singly
or in clusters; or gripped the walls with their own magnetism; or
seemed to drift, suspended, in the air, defying gravity and their
own ever threatened deflation. The longer the show-goers
looked at them, the more the works seemed to expand, engulf-
ing comic—and cosmic—truths.

Ms. Mothner called them "balloons."

Brinkley felt a tap on his shoulder.

"Nice work, eh, baby?"

It was Kojak; holding his stylish fedora; his bald head
gleaming in the gallery lights.

"I didn't know Mothner was your niece."

"Genius runs in the family," Kojak said.

They moved to the next room, to greet the artist. She threw
her thin arms around Kojak, and kissed his cheek.

"Uncle Theo! I'm glad you could come!"

"How come no baseball pictures?" he said; and winked. He
introduced Brinkley. "I used to take her to Ebbets Field when

she was a kid," he said. "She must've drawn a thousand pictures of Peewee Reese makin' the double play. And like that."

"He used to flash his badge and get us in free," Ms. Mothner said.

Brinkley himself had dreamed of being a ballplayer when he was young. Hit five hundred home runs a year. Steal three hundred bases. Catch every ball hit.

He had given up the idea. Someone might suspect something.

"I like your work very much," he said.

Ms. Mothner thanked him. Other well-wishers were waiting. They moved away. Kojak, holding a glass of champagne in one hand, shoved a Tootsie Pop into his mouth with the other. They stood in a corner, watching the socialites come and go speaking of Michael Angelo (who had just gotten divorced).

"Okay, shoot," Kojak said. "What's the big *megillah?*"

"The crime wave last night. One of the people behind it is named Stretch O'Toole. Who is he?"

"Stretch! You're kiddin'. Well I'll be an artist's uncle."

"You know him?"

"Know him?" He pulled the lollypop from his mouth. "You could say I made him what he is today."

"I'm listening."

"It was out in the Windy City. I was a rookie on the force. One night I'm walking a beat down by the docks. I hear something suspicious in the Ann-Margret Chemical Plant. A side door has been jimmied open. I draw my revolver and go inside. Two guys are stealing boxloads of chemicals. I yell 'Police!' and tell 'em to halt. One of them pulls a gun and starts shooting. I dive behind a barrel and shoot back. I wing the first guy, and he falls flat near a vat of some chemical. The other guy takes off through a window. I race outside and go after him. I collar him two blocks away. Then I come back for the first guy. He's gone. There's blood on the floor where I shot him, mixed with chemicals pouring out of bullet hole in the vat. The trail disappeared outside. I never found him. Till later."

"Later?" Brinkley said.

"You're still not with me, are ya?"

Brinkley shook his head. Kojak looked for an ashtray, to throw away his lollypop stick.

"The guy used to frequent a—how shall we say it?—a bordello, near the docks. He managed to get there. He collapsed, bleeding and unconscious. The happy hookers nursed him back to health. When he had recovered, one of the young ladies starts playing with him. Before you can say cock robin, his . . . manhood . . . is eight feet long. She faints away, of course. O'Toole reaches to pick her up, and he finds his arms can stretch, too. And his legs. The chemical in the vat had mixed with his bloodstream. He had fallen unconscious as some two-bit punk, and when he woke up he was . . ."

"Elastic Man!"

"Zapa-dapa-du," Kojak said.

Brinkley shuddered. A task far tougher than muggers lay ahead.

"I knew I knew that name. But he's never worked in New York."

"He hasn't worked anywhere, for a while. He spent a couple of weeks in the whorehouse, making the ladies happy with his newfound abilities. . . ."

"No wonder Lorna was so protective."

"What?"

"Nothing. Go on."

"Then he goes out into the big time. Robbing banks, post offices, anything he wanted. The cops were helpless. Bullets just bounced off him. And he could change into any shape he wanted, as a disguise. After a while he got bored, so he began pulling jobs in Metropolis, in Gotham. Anyplace there was a superhero to make it interesting. When the superheroes disappeared, Stretch retired, too. There were no challenges left. That's why I think you got the wrong guy, baby. What would he be doing here?"

"You'd be surprised."

"What's that supposed to mean?"

"One more question. When I called you today, the operator answered 'XYZ Industries.' Why?"

"XYZ owns Dillinger Associates. They own all the companies that hired the city cops."

"Why?"

"Why? Why? Is that all you newsmen do is ask questions? How should I know why? I suppose it wouldn't enter your liberal head that maybe they're just patriotic, or public-spirited?"

"Yeah," Brinkley said. "Maybe."

"Theo, darling!"

An elderly woman wearing too much makeup was advancing toward them. Kojak looked as if he wanted to escape; but there was no place to go. The woman hugged him, smearing makeup on his head.

It was Bubba Church. Gossip columnist for the *Catholic Yenta*.

"Who loves ya?" Kojak said.

Brinkley gave Kojak the thumbs-up sign, and moved away; through the crowded gallery; out into the street.

Darkness was falling rapidly.

On the way to the office he passed Zabar's bookstore. Its lighted window was filled with copies of a single book: *Hero,* by Norman Taylor. The publication date was not for two more weeks. The owner was cashing in on the afternoon's headlines.

Brinkley gave in quickly to the temptation, and bought a copy. He had been looking forward to it with curiosity and dread for some time. It was a biography of himself.

He carried the book through dim streets in a Zabar's bag, guiltily; as if it were smuggled dope; or something from one of the adult book bars that were springing up in the area like mumps. He might as well be carrying *Snow White and the Seven Meckies.*

Nelson Rockefeller was not outside the building. An omen that disturbed Brinkley, for no reason he could put his finger on. Freddie News was absent also. The newsstand was closed.

On the sixth floor, the city room was alive: reporters banging out their stories, the copy desk bent over its work, the wire machines clattering. Through the glass partition he could see the five o'clock news conference still in progress in Punch's office.

Racquel was sitting near the switchboard, her plum breasts proud and braless under a yellow sweater. With Pamela so pregnant he was horny for this sultry, long-haired child of nineteen.

"Hello, Racquel," he said.

"Hi, Mr. Brinkley."

It killed him every time she said that.

"Could you get me some clips from the morgue? XYZ Industries."

"Sure."

She stood, jiggling her youth and health.

He stumbled, and banged his knee painfully on the desk.

Sprawling aureoles, bright pink. With a small mole near the cleavage.

He couldn't help it.

"Are you all right?" she asked.

He nodded. She turned, and walked toward the morgue. Firm buttocks, a matching mole on the left, near the crack.

He walked into a pillar, banging his head. The book was jarred from his hand.

Bob Woodward, passing nearby, said, "Three-martini lunch?"

Brinkley gathered up the book without replying. He walked to a desk at the rear of the room, and sat down. A copy-desk drunk. That's what they would all think of him if he kept this up.

He pulled the book from the bag. A red cover, with his emblem in white in the center, half-hidden by a purple mask. Nice. And fat. Six hundred pages of the glories of his past. Or Norman Taylor's assessment of those glories. He turned to the introduction, and began to read:

• • •

Aquarius, in his 57 rutting years, had mounted many an eager female thigh: fleshy or firm, suntanned or pale, muscular from tennis or soft from chocolates in bed; had by his own count skewered four wives and four score other ladies (four score and seven to be exact, a patriotic coincidence). Four wives and 87 nonwives (some of them, to be sure, other people's wives). Using a pocket calculator, and conservative estimates—750 penetrations per wife, three penetrations per nonwife—he had arrived at a total of more than 2,500 penetrations in all, not counting the whores of his adolescence. On those occasions, he had performed satisfactorily, by his own reckoning, a solid 89 percent of the time (depending, as they say at swim meets, on the degree of difficulty of the dive).

With such a batting average, if metaphors may be mixed, he had no real reason to be concerned with his prowess. But he was. Because in every one of those 2,500-odd penetrations—some of them odder than others—as the moment of climax approached, his thoughts were not of himself, nor of the female partner sweating and writhing below (or above, or beside) him. His thoughts at that dread moment, without exception, were of a caped figure in a purple mask, immortal, infinite in strength, sublime in the variety of his powers—the familiar hero of superheroes. Aquarius, never one to underestimate his own abilities, nevertheless found at the hard-core moments of his being this wish to be someone else: this masked Phoenix who by the nature of his powers could stay potent longer, pump longer, ejaculate longer than any other creature on Earth.

In time, there being no other choice, Aquarius had come to accept this intruder in his bedroom. At times even to welcome him as a helpful partner in the prolonging of the sex act. But, freed from the urgencies of the bed, his intellect like a separate being began to ponder the phenomenon. How had this being from a dead planet come to occupy so central a place in American mythology, in the American psyche? So central a place that he lived not only in the fantasies of children but in the very glands and pores and organs of Aquarius; and by extension (since Aquarius did not consider himself a freak) in the glands and pores and organs of the American race?

This mysterious superhero, at once sophisticated and naive, had clearly risen above the calling of catcher of crooks, defender of the helpless. He had become in the mind of man—and, Aquarius had it on good authority, in the mind of woman as well—the universal Superstud. He had staked his claim in that battered part of the human heart reserved for sexual nirvana. He lived, in short, a hop, skip and jump away from our souls.

Perceived in this way, the hero became a fit subject for the *typewriter of Aquarius: to explore his origins, his deeds, the symbolic meaning of his acts, the overwhelming fact of his sudden disappearance. So Aquarius decided to explore those questions in an essay of modest length.*

The result, three years later, is this book of nearly a million words. Aquarius came to feel, during his investigations, that his subject was well worth—even demanded—such serious and lengthy consideration. He can only hope that the reader will agree.

• • •

Brinkley sensed a figure looming above him.

"Here're your clips," Racquel said.

"Thanks."

He took the folder, and watched her retreating down the aisle. Postpubescent poetry in motion.

He closed the book. There it was again. Himself as Superstud. Peggy's fixation of twenty years ago. Made immortal history now by Norman Taylor.

If only they knew the truth! If only they knew that as his superself he couldn't get it up!

He had gone to a psychiatrist about it, back then. In the days when Peggy would lie beside him and long for a superfuck. For his other self.

He had gotten the name from the Yellow Pages. Dr. J. Carouthers—Shrink—Three Couches, No Waiting—Am Ex, DC, MC—You Saw Me on the Carson Show.

He could not go as Brinkley, of course. It was the same as with the tailor. He had to go in uniform; because that was when the problem arose.

Or failed to arise.

He had called up, and made an appointment under a name he chose at random from the phone book. Gregory Peck.

The building was on Park Avenue. He stripped to his uniform in the basement, and stepped onto the elevator. The doors closed. They opened again at the lobby floor. A gray-haired woman got in. She was carrying a white poodle. The poodle was dressed in a blue jacket, and purple pants. It had red ribbons over its ears.

The woman turned, and looked at Brinkley. She stepped off the elevator before the doors closed.

He got off at the eleventh floor, and entered an office marked "Crazies." A receptionist was behind a desk.

"I'm Gregory Peck," Brinkley said. "I have an appointment with Dr. Carouthers."

"I'm Humphrey Bogart," the receptionist said. "Won't you have a seat?"

He stared, hard, through the eye-holes of his mask, at the receptionist. She didn't look at all like Humphrey Bogart. Brinkley wasn't sure if he was being mocked.

He sat in a plastic armchair. A plain-looking woman, seated across from him, took no notice. A door opened, and a man emerged from an inner office. He was dressed like Napoleon. He took the woman's arm, and they left.

Maybe every shrink has one, Brinkley thought. Like a cigar-store Indian.

The receptionist peered into the inner office, then turned.

"You can go in now, Mr. Peck."

Brinkley stood, and entered the office. He stopped short, surprised. The doctor was a woman. He moved in, and sat in a leather armchair facing the desk.

"I'm Gregory Peck," he said.

"I'm Joyce Carouthers," the doctor said.

"Actually," Brinkley said, "I'm not really Gregory Peck. You can see who I really am. But I live under a secret identity that I can't reveal. I just borrowed the name Gregory Peck so you'd have something to call me."

"Pity," the doctor said. "I was creaming all morning."

"I beg your pardon?"

"No matter. What is your problem, Mr. Pecker?"

"That's Peck."

"Peck. I'm sorry."

"My problem involves sex," Brinkley said.

Dr. Carouthers smiled. "I was hoping it would."

"In my secret identity—as Gregory Peck—I have no problem with sex."

"I should think not," the doctor said.

"But as my superself, I . . . I . . ." He hesitated, blushing.

"Don't be shy, Mr. Pecker. Think of me not as a woman but as a doctor. My interest in this is strictly clinical."

"I know that, doctor. What I mean to say is, as my superself, I can't seem to get an . . . erection."

Dr. Carouthers placed her elbows on the desk. Her fingers were laced together under her chin, pensively.

"Not even when some horny cunt is licking your balls?"

"Not even then."

"I see," the doctor said. She made some notes on a stenographic pad in front of her. "Do you have any idea yourself about what is causing this problem?"

"I've thought about it a lot," Brinkley said. "I think it's a fear of failure. A fear of not being good enough. In my secret identity, women see me as an ordinary man. They don't expect too much. So I function adequately. But when they see me in my uniform, they expect me to be the greatest . . ."

"Fucker?"

". . . in the world. And I know I'm just average. So I can't even get it started. Because I know I'll disappoint them."

The doctor made more notes. "I wasn't going to comment on your costume," she said. "But as long as you brought it up, let's talk about that. Why do you dress like that? From what you've said, that seems to be the heart of your problem. If you didn't dress like that, there would be no heightened expectations."

Brinkley looked at her. She did not seem to be joking.

"I have to dress this way," he said, a touch of anger creeping into his voice. "I'm a superhero. This is what superheroes wear."

The doctor's pen raced quickly across her pad.

"How long have you been a superhero?" she said.

"What do you mean, how long? Always. I was born this way."

"You were born superior to everyone else?"

"If that's the way you want to put it—yes!"

His breath was coming quickly, his heartbeat pounding in his chest. He had never been forced to speak this way before.

"I see," the doctor said.

She stood, and looked out the window behind her at the pale towers of the city. For a full minute neither of them spoke. Then the doctor turned to face him.

"It seems to me, Mr. Pecker . . ."

"Peck!"

". . . Mr. Peck, that your own interpretation of your inadequacy might be a bit too conventional. Too simplistic. Let's try another hypothesis. Isn't it possible that when you are in costume—when you are a superhero, as you put it—you feel that you are better than everyone else? That no woman lying beside you—however beautiful and alluring she may be—is good enough for you? That because the woman is a mere mortal, whereas you are a superior being, that you have decided subconsciously to punish her inferiority by withholding from her the pleasures of your erect penis? By withholding your . . . super . . . seed?"

"I . . . I don't know. I never thought about it that way."

"Perhaps we should begin thinking about it that way, Mr. Pecker."

"My name is not Pecker! It's Gregory Peck!"

"But you told me before that your name was not Gregory Peck. That you had merely borrowed that name. If that is the case, what difference is it what I call you?"

"I guess that's true," Brinkley said, lamely. He couldn't believe what was happening. He felt as if he were being battered by a superior intellect.

The doctor sat down in her chair.

"I think we should begin again," she said. "If I am to be able to help you, there has to be a relationship of trust between us. You can begin that trust by telling me your real name.''

Brinkley was silent. His emotions warred within him. He wanted to trust this doctor. He wanted desperately to solve his problem. But no mortal being knew his identity. If it were ever to be revealed, his supercareer would be ended. Any stray villain could hold his mortal friends hostage. Or any future family he might have.

''I can't,'' he said.

The doctor frowned. ''I'm afraid you'll have to,'' she said, ''if you want me to help you overcome this superiority complex.''

Brinkley's eyes narrowed.

''What complex? I don't have a complex.''

''This superhero fixation, then,'' the doctor said. ''Call it what you will.''

He stared at her. ''You don't believe me,'' he said. ''You think I'm some kind of crazy nut, running around in a cape and tights. Like that loony Napoleon who just walked out.''

''Mr. Wilson is a lovely man,'' the doctor said. ''He's on the board of education. As for yourself, I didn't say crazy, and I didn't say nut. Those were your words.''

''But that's what you were thinking!''

''Not at all.''

Brinkley slumped in the chair, his hope of help slipping away. He rubbed his mask with his hands. Then he sat upright.

''You said a minute ago that for this to work, we need mutual trust. Is that right?''

''That's right,'' the doctor said.

''Okay. I'll make a deal with you. I'll trust you, if you trust me. I'll tell you my secret identity—something I've never told anyone—something that can put me in great danger—if you'll believe me when I say I'm a superhero.''

''Now we're getting somewhere. It's a deal.''

''Good,'' Brinkley said.

He stood. He moved past the desk, to the window.

''What are you doing?''

He opened the window, as high as it would go. Cool air rushed in. He turned and faced the doctor.

"Jump," he said.

"What?"

"Jump out the window. I'll catch you."

The doctor's face reddened. She grew flustered.

"I can't do that."

"Don't you believe I can fly?"

"It's not that," she stammered. "I'm afraid of heights. A neurosis."

"You should get help," Brinkley said.

He pondered a moment. Then he said, "Okay. *I'll* jump."

He placed his foot on the radiator. He hoisted himself onto the sill. Slowly he moved out onto the ledge.

The doctor watched him, transfixed. And then panicked. She leaped out of her chair, frantic. She rushed to the window, and wrapped both her arms around his knees.

"Humphrey!" she shrieked.

The receptionist came rushing in, and grabbed him, one hand around his hip, the other between his legs. He feigned resistance, and let the two women drag him back inside, down onto the floor. The receptionist threw her weight across him. She lay on top of him, holding him down, while the doctor closed the window and locked it. The sensation was not at all unpleasant. Humphrey Bogart had big tits.

"It's okay now," the doctor said.

The receptionist pretended not to hear.

"I said it's okay now!"

Reluctantly, the receptionist climbed off, straightening her skirt. Brinkley stood, slowly, adjusting his cape, wiping plaster dust from his blue tights. Blue showed everything.

He smiled shyly at the receptionist; and then, in a different way, at the doctor.

"So much for trust," he said.

Neither woman spoke. He walked by them, out of the office, down the hall; past a woman dressed as Marie Antoinette.

He could feel their eyes on him as he waited for the elevator.

He could have flown away, out the window. And proved who he really was. He wouldn't give them the satisfaction.

In the elevator, he felt his tights pressed heavily against his groin. He had an erection! Humphrey Bogart had succeeded where a dozen naked *majas* had failed.

He pondered the phenomenon. Sex through violence! No more Mr. Nice Guy! A whole new world spread invitingly before him.

He never had the nerve to try it.

The shuffling of feet in the city room brought him back to the present. The news conference had ended, the editors were moving back to their desks. He shoved the Taylor book into a drawer, and pulled a thick wad of clippings from the envelope Racquel had brought him.

He glanced through the clips quickly: stories about space probes, synthetic chemicals, the building industry, food packaging, highway construction, furniture design. Every aspect of modern life seemed to be represented. He found a long piece that had appeared in the Sunday business section, reviewing the spectacular growth of XYZ Industries since its founding ten years earlier. Alongside the article was a list of companies owned or controlled by XYZ:

Prather Tool Co.
Halligan Steel
Kwartler Bank and Trust
Payne Aeronautics
Kampel Aerospace
McCord Plastics
Amster Minerals and Mining
Mullan Copper
Schwartz Laboratories
Vecsey Aluminum
Richards-Jessup Carbide
Isaacs Electronics

Salzberg Trucking
Ziegel Farms
Clifford Pipe and Tubing
Amsel Research
Oppenheimer Glass Works
Cohen Wax
Koblin Fabrics
Chapin Mills
Constable-on-Call
Pintz Detection Agency
Hart Plumbing Works
Dravo Porcelain
Friedman Paints
Pisacane Restaurant Supply Co.
Jacobson Drugs
Halperin Laundries
Weiss Security
Rokoff Protection Services
Eli's Night Watchmen
Dillinger Associates

He stared at the list, trying to discern some pattern that might apply to his own life. There were a high proportion of recently acquired security agencies, which had hired the city cops. But beyond that?

An amorphous thought, a large concept like a vaporous cloud, began drifting in and out of his head; too large and too . . . whimsical—a curious word, but the one that occurred to him—too large and whimsical to be fully grasped; let alone believed. He would reach for it, and it would change shape, one thought puffing out and losing itself in another. Leaving him empty-handed. Empty-headed.

His eye fell on a paragraph high up in the story: "Although XYZ Industries is a major conglomerate, it is only part of a still larger industrial octopus. It is a wholly-owned subsidiary of Powell Pugh Enterprises, one of the largest multinational corporations in the world."

He absorbed the information in the computer of his brain, and pushed a button. No neat answer came out. Only more questions.

He needed to go to the bathroom. The lavatory nearest the city room had been closed for a week, being renovated, but now it was back in use. He pushed the door open, into the smell of wet paint.

He used a urinal, and washed his hands. The shiny faucet knobs were marked "Hart Plumbing." The bathroom started to move, circling around him. He grabbed at the sink, to steady himself. An ink tattoo on the edge said "Dravo Porcelain." He grew dizzier. He began to lose his balance.

He turned on a tap, and splashed cold water on his face.

The water hit his eyes and nose and mouth like a sledge hammer.

He spun away from the impact, grabbing his face.

And crumpled to the tile floor in a dead faint.

Presidential assistant Richard C. "Bugs" Bunny escorted Paul Vincent through the corridors of the White House, to the family living quarters on the second floor. The president had been in conference all afternoon with the Emperor of Japan, and was preparing to attend a state dinner at night. Bunny, hearing the urgency of Vincent's voice on the phone, had agreed to let him come over while the president was dressing. Now, as he knocked on the bedroom door, he was having second thoughts.

"This better be good," Bunny said, "or we're both in trouble."

The door was opened by the president's valet, Fred Astaire. (The president liked men around him who had rhythm.)

Bunny followed Vincent into the room. Vincent turned, and said, more sharply than he had intended, "This is for the president's ears only."

Bunny flushed scarlet, hesitated, and left the room; thinking that it was true what they said about Vincent. He didn't know his place.

Bugs Bunny, Vincent was thinking, has big ears.

The president was nowhere in sight. The valet went to a closet, and began laying evening clothes on the bed: top hat, white tie, and tails. Vincent scanned the room: the ornate furniture, the portrait of Lincoln looking down sadly from the wall, the brass plaque on the footboard of the bed that said "Judith Campbell Exner Slept Here."

The stately quiet was broken by the flushing of a toilet. A door opened, and the president emerged from the bathroom, wearing an orange terrycloth robe. Vincent noticed that he had hairy legs.

"Evening, Mr. President," Vincent said.

"Hello, Vincent. What the hell is so urgent it couldn't wait till morning?"

Vincent looked at the valet.

"That's all, Fred," the president said.

The valet glided gracefully to the door, and closed it behind him.

"Well?" the president said.

"Are we being taped?"

"Who do you think I am, Nixon?"

"Are we?"

The president approached the four-poster bed, and twisted the knob of one of the posts.

"Not now," he said. "My word."

Vincent nodded, and began the recital he had been rehearsing in his head for the past two hours. About the first approach, and his refusal. About Mortimer's illness, and the bills. About the second approach, and how he had agreed. He stated it flatly, dryly, not looking for sympathy.

The president remained silent. He walked to the bathroom, and began lathering his face with soap. He left the door open.

"Who is this mysterious agent you've been running?"

Vincent stood in the doorway to the bathroom.

"He was recruited—bought would be more accurate—at an oil conference in Vienna, by some Dallas superpatriot. For millions in a Swiss bank. It's . . ." His voice wavered. He fought to keep it steady. ". . . Werner von Oskar."

The president looked at him, his face covered with lather, and raised an eyebrow. He pursed his lips, getting lather on them. And nodded.

"The Russian foreign minister himself? Why?"

"Because of garlic."

(The Soviet-American disarmament talks were known formally as the General Armaments Reduced-Level Inventory Conference. GARLIC, for short.)

"Explain," the president said.

"I assumed the purpose was to delay disarmament. Dallas didn't want it. There's too much money in munitions. So they had von Oskar raise the . . . Indigo issue." He was careful to use the code, even here. "The death of Indigo as a secret precondition to disarmament. If you went along with it, they would be rid of Indigo, who they've always hated. An eastern liberal superhero. If you didn't go along with it, GARLIC would be delayed indefinitely. They'd win either way."

The president washed the soap from his face, and began applying lather from an aerosol can.

"You're saying that the Indigo demand originated in Dallas? That the Russian high command merely agreed to go along with it?"

"I'm saying the Russian leaders don't even know about it. It's all Dallas and von Oskar. Von Oskar has been lying to his bosses about the delay. Saying you just don't want to disarm."

"The Kremlin isn't worried about Indigo?"

"The Kremlin has never seen Indigo, so they don't believe he exists. It's like God. They think he's an American invention."

The president rinsed his razor, and began to shave. He talked into the mirror.

"So we can go ahead with disarmament," he said. "Why are you telling me this now?"

"I'm not finished," Vincent said. "Dallas bought von Oskar, right? They convinced Van Buren they had the interests of the country at heart. Van Buren blackmailed me into running von Oskar for them. Simple, so far, But Van Buren was afraid von Oskar might pull a double-cross. Work for the Russians as a double agent. So he put a close-up watch on von Oskar."

"And that was . . .?"

"The interpreter, Yakov. A long-time deep-cover man."

They were interrupted by the ringing of a phone near the bed. The president answered it.

"Hello? Yes . . . His name is Hirohito. . . . Not Hero
Hito . . . One word."

He slammed the phone onto the hook.

"Goddammed Edward Bear. 'Make me a speechwriter,' he said. Christ! Where were we?"

"About Yakov," Vincent said. "He confronted von Oskar
with the evidence that he had sold out. Von Oskar turned white.
Then Yakov confessed that he, too, was a spy. It established a
confidence between them. It sealed a bond. But it also gave
Yakov two seats on the fifty-yard line. What von Oskar was
saying and doing in Moscow. And what Van Buren was telling
him from here. Gradually he began to suspect there was more to
this than a delay in GARLIC."

"How do you know this?"

Vincent allowed himself a modest pause; and a modest look
at his shoes. Then he looked up again.

"Yakov is my man," he said. "From Berlin."

The president completed shaving, in a silence broken only
by the running water. He wiped his face with a towel marked
Acapulco Hilton, and reentered the bedroom.

"I still don't see the sudden urgency of this confessional."

"The trouble in New York," Vincent said. "It smelled bad
from the beginning. Like some kind of plot. But against whom?
I couldn't figure it. I said, let's start with the top. Suppose it
were against the president. Who would stand to gain? The first
answer was Bub . . . the vice president."

The president sat in his rocking chair, and motioned Vincent
to an easy chair nearby.

"Go on," he said.

"That seemed unlikely. But you've got to check everything.
So I called Bascomb. Luckily he was home. I invited him and
his wife to a late supper. Candice whipped up something in a
hurry." He smiled. "That was the hard part. Convincing Candice to have them, without telling her why. She can't stand Bascomb."

"Stick to the point," the president said.

"We talked alone in the garden after dinner. I wanted to see if he knew anything. I led him on, letting him think I knew more than I did. Obviously he knew from Van Buren that I knew something. He bit. He spilled the whole thing. It all ties in."

"Meaning what?"

"Meaning the plot in New York is against Indigo. Since you wouldn't go along with it, Indigo is to be killed by henchmen of Dallas. As soon as he shows himself."

"Paul, I think you've been playing spy too long. If Indigo is killed, they defeat their own purposes. They remove the last obstacle to GARLIC—an obstacle you say they themselves created."

"Correct," Vincent said. "And what can we infer from that? One. That they raised the Indigo death issue because they really want him out of the way, so he can't mess up their future plans. Two. That the disarmament treaty will then be signed. But we know they don't want disarmament. And why would they let Bascomb in on it? There's only one answer that makes sense. Once the treaty is signed, they plan to have you killed. Bubblehead will become president. A puppet in the Oval Office. Publicly, he'll make a show of disarming. But they'll keep secret stockpiles. Once the Russians disarm, Dallas will rule the world."

"That's mostly conjecture," the president said.

"It's the only logical answer."

The president stood, and paced the room. The phone rang again.

"Hello? Japan! Not China! He's the emperor of Japan. Dammit."

He hung up, angrily.

"A speechwriter of Very Little Brain," he said.

"Why did you hire him?"

"A favor to Congressman Robin. Where were we?"

"Bubblehead."

"Disarmament," the president said. "If we expose von Oskar as a fraud, we can go ahead with disarmament."

"Then Dallas will have you killed."

"I'll have to take my chances. Disarmament is crucial, before someone blows up the planet. But the first thing we have to do is warn Indigo that New York is a trap."

"No," Vincent said.

"What do you mean, no?"

"If we warn him—and he doesn't show himself—they'll know he's too weak to stop them. They'll move ahead. But if he comes out into the open, at least they'll expose their hand, and you can move against them."

"But if he's weak, they'll kill him. You said so yourself."

"A sacrifice for the country," Vincent said.

The president stopped pacing. He placed his hand on Vincent's shoulder, then let it drop.

"I admire what you've done," he said. "I appreciate your tough-mindedness. But is that how you want the country run? Let good men walk into traps? Men who have done so much?"

For the first time, Vincent didn't know what to say. He felt sheepish. He had underestimated the president.

"It's all talk, anyway," he said. "There's no way we can locate Indigo, until he shows himself. By then it might be too late."

"You may be right," the president said. He picked up the phone near the bed. "On the other hand, you may be wrong." He cupped his hand over the receiver. "You never heard what you're about to hear."

Vincent nodded.

"Get me New York," the president said. "The Anastasia Hotel. I want to speak to Miss Peggy Poole."

The president held the phone, waiting.

"Perhaps you should go now, Vincent," he said. "Thank you for your information. I'll keep in touch."

"I'll help in any way I can," Vincent said.

He crossed the room, and opened the bedroom door. As he was leaving, he looked back. Someone apparently had answered the phone in New York. A large white toothy smile lit the president's black face.

Brinkley's head ached. He felt like a cartoon character konked on the head with a two-by-four or a falling safe. His thoughts rose in blank white circles; wordless smoke signals screaming in a fog.

A face was looking down at him.

"What happened?"

He felt cold leather under his palms. A sofa.

"You fainted."

Ellipses of passing time rolled across the floor, like marbles.

"When?"

"A few minutes ago."

He remembered going to the bathroom. Feeling dizzy. Splashing water on his face. The names of companies on the plumbing.

He sat up, slowly. Time skittered like cartoon mice along the wall.

"You feel okay?"

He nodded.

"Maybe it wasn't a good idea," Punch said. "Going back on the streets."

"I'll be all right. I just need some rest."

His head was clearing. Pale fire burning away the fog.

"Take the night off, if you want."

"Maybe."

He stood, and left Punch's office, shakily; an idea bouncing like a silver pinball through his brain, lighting up first one lobe, then another, till he could almost feel his feverish forehead spelling TILT. He returned to his desk, and reread the list of XYZ's holdings; memorizing it. He read other clippings—accounts of space probes ten years earlier. Then he took the box he had been carrying all afternoon—the box Max had given him—and left the building.

The lobby was deserted. The streets were emptying quickly, people hurrying from midtown in the falling darkness. Time running on commuter feet to the suburbs, before the muggers came out. Postwar America in microcosm. National Guardsmen stood with fixed bayonets on every corner.

The cloud that had been drifting through his brain distilled into sharper focus. He was beginning to see how they could have done it. But it was too mammoth a conceit. The whole world did not revolve around him; much as he sometimes liked to think so.

A ten-year plot against himself? It was too much to believe. What was the motive?

He remembered his discovery of the afternoon: that his strength seemed to vary with his location. He felt strongest amid the old tenements of the Lower East Side. And underground, in the subway, with its dilapidated equipment. He felt weakest amid the modern buildings of midtown, and out in the suburbs.

It fit the theory. Still . . .

The pilot light of anger was warming the back of his neck. For eight years he had lived comfortably, if unheroically, in the suburbs, while the city went to ruin. Crime rampant in the streets. The middle class moving out. Slum areas spreading, buildings being abandoned. The tax base shrinking. Businesses moving away. Unemployment rising, welfare rising, the downward spiral intensifying, feeding upon itself; the city heading toward bankruptcy. People blamed the mayor, and past mayors. They blamed the blacks, and the Puerto Ricans. They blamed the state, and the federal government, for taking the city's money in taxes and not giving enough back.

All of it specious reasoning. A refusal to face the obvious, to state the unthinkable: that the city started going downhill when it lost its superhero. When it lost him.

It was *his* strong hand that had kept New York functioning all those years; *his* shadow in the skies that kept street crime in check; that interposed itself between businessmen-politicians and the corruption they craved; that held out the hope of justice to the oppressed. When his familiar cape and mask vanished from the scene, the balance wheel was broken. The city plummeted.

He could not blame himself. His weakness was real, not psychological; a betrayal by nature, or the gods. Or so it had seemed. Till now.

Now he had to rethink it all. Was it really possible that the past eight years had not simply happened to him, but had *been done* to him?

O villain, villain, smiling, damned villain!

(Hamlet. One of his Top-Three princes.)

He turned into the lobby of the Anastasia Hotel. It was a decrepit place, past its prime; the kind of midtown hotel tourists no longer frequented. The carpet was threadbare, the walls were peeling.

Each evidence of its decay gave him comfort.

He registered at the desk, and signed for a package addressed to Peggy that was on the counter. They were together, he said. A sullen bellhop, Gerald Ford, took the boxes.

"Easy with those," the desk clerk said.

"Drop dead," Ford replied.

In his room he tested the water, gingerly. It seemed okay. He peeled off his clothing and his grungy uniform, and took a hot shower, and looked at his naked flesh in the mirror—flesh and muscle that had withstood the most powerful evils in the universe. And beyond. Flesh gone flabby with time.

His anger flared higher. In the old days he would have plowed to the center of it, fists flying. He was lean, hard, tough. Now he would have to control it. Remain civilized. Yet somehow drag his being into action.

He opened the box Max had given him, and put on the outfit. It felt strange. Like a clown's. He opened the second box, and pulled his brand-new uniform over the other. Dressing for whatever battles might lie ahead.

Or for his funeral.

A perfect fit. Max was still a wizard with a needle.

He unsnapped the pocket in the cape where he felt paper rustling, expecting to find the bill. Instead there was only a two-word note, in Max's uncertain scrawl. It said, "Heppy Hunting."

He shook his head, and smiled.

The uniform was so clean. It would not be that way for long. If enough muggers attacked him at once, they could tear it apart.

They could tear *him* apart.

He thought of Goober. Something Goober had said contained the kernel of a plan. A way out. What was it?

Of course!

He looked at his watch. Time beating in the blood of his wrist. He put on his clothing quickly. He would have to hurry.

He dialed Peggy's room. The line was busy. He called the desk, and left a message. He would meet her at Elaine's at seven.

He left the hotel, and flagged a cab.

"Where to?" Bella Abzug said.

"Tinkerbell's."

During the ride Abzug kept glancing at him surreptitiously in the rear-view miror. Tinkerbell's was a hangout for gays.

The hell with that. He would recruit superhelp wherever he could find it.

He tapped his foot impatiently at a red light. Time plus distance equals cabfare. The last urban certainty.

Tinkerbell's was crowded, with men standing three-deep at the bar. Most of them neat, manicured. There was not a woman in sight. He edged through to the front, and caught the eye of the bartender.

"I'm looking for Peter," he said.

"Who isn't?" a man next to him said, and touched Brinkley's groin.

Brinkley shoved the hand away, roughly.

"Oooh. A regular blue-haired ape," the man said.

Brinkley followed the bartender's nod toward a booth at the rear. He worked his way there. Peter was writing in a ledger. They shook hands, warmly. Brinkley sat across from him.

Their words were lost in the chatter of the bar.

"Will you look at that," the man at the bar said, sipping his daiquiri. "Peter gets all the good ones."

He continued to watch them, giving a running account to the bartender.

"Blue-boy is leaning over, whispering to him. . . . Peter is smiling. . . . Oh my God. Blue-boy is giving Peter his hotel key. And Peter is taking it! And nodding! Well I'll be . . . It didn't take him but two minutes. . . . Will you look at that! They're gonna leave together."

They hurried outside, and waved down a cab.

"You take it," Brinkley said. "I'm going the other way."

Peter climbed in, and the cab left the curb. Brinkley hailed another.

"I don't believe this," he said. "This is absurd."

"Call me Bella," the driver said.

He got out at Elaine's, which was crowded as usual with celebrities: John Smith, Jane Doe, Jack Public. All the biggies. He sat at the bar and ordered a ginger ale—there would be no more drinking tonight—and waited impatiently for Peggy.

The old excitement at seeing her mingled with his apprehension about the night ahead. After twenty years, the image of her lying naked on her sofa was as vivid as if it had been last night. It made his loins ache. Her large breasts with the nipples that seemed to reach out, the incredible softness of her thighs, the Indian-black hair disappearing between them.

His first love. A love never properly consummated, despite all their nakedness.

As long as he lived, that would be his regret. An eighteen-minute gap in his being.

She arrived a few minutes later, breathless and pale; and ordered a Dewar's.

"It's terrible," she said, her voice carrying below the barroom noise. "A plot to kill him! We've got to find him!"

"Wait a minute, slow down," he said. "What are you talking about?"

She told him of the call from the president; the international intrigue; the plot by Dallas to enslave the world. Beginning with his own death. Not knowing it was him, of course.

"O, villain, villain . . ." he murmured, mournfully. Time dripping wetly into his lap. Sticky, like ginger ale.

"David! You're bleeding!"

In his growing tension he had squeezed the glass to pieces. Ginger ale was running off the bar. A thin line of blood had spurted at the base of his thumb. He pulled out his handkerchief, and wiped his pants; and the blood.

The last piece of the puzzle! The motive. The plot against him only a start toward a worldwide takeover.

It made sense. He couldn't try to pretend any longer that it wasn't happening.

He peered at his injured thumb. Two options lay before him. One was not to show up. Let the muggers run free. Few people would get hurt. The midtown area was almost deserted. Let the plot run its course. If the president knew about it, perhaps it could be defused. The FBI. The CIA. Mary Worth. Someone could handle it. He could go on living his life as before. As if nothing had happened. David Brinkley, private citizen.

The bolder—dumber?—choice was to fight. To strip down to his uniform and meet them head-on, as best he could. Using his wits, and whatever poor strength he could summon. Hoping that his guess as to how they had done it was correct. To destroy them some way—or die trying.

Leaving Pamela and the girls alone. With the baby coming.

For the first time he envied the Captain in his sanitarium. Beyond the reach of worldly pulls.

He knew what he wanted to do. He wanted to fade back out of the picture; to lie snugly in Peggy's—Pamela's!—arms; to say to hell with the world. What difference to Brinkley if the world was governed by corrupt Washington, or corrupt Dallas? Bread and sunshine would smell the same. He had given enough in the service of man. No more comic-book heroics.

He knew, also, what he was going to do. His Cronko-Puritan conscience wouldn't let him run.

"I'm not hungry," Peggy said. "I've lost my appetite."

"Me too. Let's go. I think I know where he is."

Time ticking in the mechanisms of bombs.

"Where?"

"Where the muggers are. Reuben Goober told me. Probably told him, too, when he was arrested."

They didn't have to flag a cab. Abzug was waiting at the curb.

"You in on this plot?" Brinkley said.

"What?"

"Never mind. Pier Fifty-two. And step on it."

A bright full moon washed the squat, brooding buildings of the warehouse district. The foghorns of tugs on the river seemed mere exhibitionism: the posturing of gray peahens. The West Side Highway stood silhouetted on stanchions of one-legged birds. Stray traffic overhead like the beating of wings.

Bird images, Brinkley noted. Psychic tricks. Apprehension about returning to the air. Becoming a bird of prey. Or pray. Flying could be fearsome at times. That's why birds shit white.

"There's the warehouse," Brinkley said. "We better wait here."

They were across the street from the entrance. He prayed that Peter was in place.

"Look, the doors are opening," Peggy said. "We got here just in time."

A rectangle of light had appeared across the street. Forms of men began to emerge from it, in an endless stream.

"Let's get out of here," he said. "Those guys are dangerous."

"You kidding? This is the story!"

She hadn't changed.

"I don't know about you, but I'm leaving."

He scooted around the corner, out of sight. Once more

branding the *c* of cowardice upon his head. An occupational hazard.

He slipped into a doorway, and stripped to his uniform. He stuffed his clothing in the pocket of the cape. And fastened on his purple mask.

The return to battle, after all these years. The moment of truth.

He grabbed an empty trash can from a cluster near the curb, and carried it up three flights of fire escape steps to the roof. (He dared not fly with it; he might drop the thing.) On the roof he removed the bottom of the can with a swift kick. Thank Nietzsche they had chosen the decaying warehouse district, he thought. Here he still could muster some strength.

"OKAY. STOP WHERE YOU ARE!"

He was standing on a low brick wall that rimmed the roof, using the trash can as a megaphone. The bright moon showed him off in Max's glorious threads to the muggers milling below. He knew he looked spectacular in his cape, mask, tights, the weird emblem on his chest. He felt the old pride returning.

The muggers were startled by the voice booming in the night. They stopped in the street, hundreds of them, and milled about, those who had spotted his form pointing him out to others.

"RETURN TO YOUR HOMES AT ONCE."

They didn't move. But he had all their attention now. A thousand of them, standing in the street, looking up at him. A moment's pause before their vile mission began.

Sometimes he was convinced there was a factory under the earth that turned out muggers. Under Central Park, perhaps. A churning, clanging factory filthy with skin and rags and hair, molding refuse into human shapes. The models perfected and shipped up through the sewers into the streets. Moral lepers with terminal mind-filth. Addicts of blood with switchblade fangs. Spitters and coughers and white-suited nose-pickers (sticking their snot on the nearest passing face, pissing on the floors of the museums). Shooters of bullets into the spines of innocents. A million nasty tricks, and they learned them all at the factory, everything from whispered sucks to slashed aortas (blades available by mail from *Today's Mugger*). The factory crunching the insane into faceless dregs, vomiting them up in the dark. A diseased army conquering, holding greasy flags aloft (gonorrhea on a field of lice). Mindless, mindless, innocent of nice. Until the streets were theirs; and decent folk could only break and run.

It made him angry sometimes.

He imagined himself finding this underground factory. Smashing it apart with his powerful fists. Destroying it utterly.

One of his Top-Three fantasies.

Unfortunately, it was not that simple.

He looked down at them, milling in the street; their foreheads wan in the moonlight, like balloons with slow leaks.

"RETURN TO YOUR HOMES," he said again.

"Says who?" one of them yelled. "You a has-been. An old man. You can't even fly."

Others in the crowd snickered.

He set the trash can down. The moment of truth, plus one.

"Dumbo!" he shouted—the prearranged signal—and leaped into the air. He hovered momentarily over the building; then dove. He disappeared behind the low wall on the roof.

With perfect timing, Peter soared from his hiding place, and darted down at them, like a missile. The crowd gasped as one. Back and forth Peter flew, quick as a hummingbird, menacing as a hawk—Peter Pan in Brinkley's spare uniform and mask, pulled tight with safety pins to fit his smaller form. Peter who in the darkest days of Brinkley's early weakness had taught him to think Good Thoughts before flying. It made for smoother take-offs.

Back and forth he darted and glided above them, his blonde hair darkened with ashes. They gave ground, melted backward against the outer wall of the warehouse. Confused comments drifted up to the roof.

"Son of a bitch!"

"Who said he couldn't fly?"

"I ain't tangling with him."

Peter soared high, and landed on the roof, dropping behind the wall. Brinkley stood, holding the trash can.

"SO MUCH FOR FLYING. DISPERSE QUIETLY. THE FUN AND GAMES ARE OVER."

"Oh yeah?" came a voice from the crowd. "So maybe you can fly. So can a sparrow fly. Let's see if you can fight!"

"ANY VOLUNTEERS?" he said.

Most of them pressed tighter against the wall.

"HOW ABOUT YOU?" he said, pointing.

A murmur of fear ran through the crowd of muggers. He set down the trash can, and leaped down to the street. He ran at them, and yanked at a fellow on the edge of the crowd. He pulled him into full view, about twenty feet in front of them.

"Say your prayers," he said.

"No, don't hit me," the fellow pleaded, in a voice pitched high with fear.

"You should have thought of that before," Brinkley said.

He pulled back his fist, slowly, dramatically. And slammed it forward as hard as he could; grunting. "Biff! Bam!"

In the semidarkness of the street they couldn't see that he pulled the punches just before they landed, slamming his fist with a crunch into his own hand.

The crunch sent the fellow flying, backward, head over heels, high into the air; tumbling like a tin can in the bright light of the moon. He seemed to hang suspended in the air a moment, like a pop fly. Then he came tumbling down, and landed with a sickening thud on the roof.

Brinkley summoned his strength, and leaped up to the roof after him. He picked up the trash can. He didn't really need it, but it made his voice more menacing.

"THAT'S ONE," he said. "ANY MORE TAKERS?"

There was silence in the street.

"OKAY. WALK SLOWLY TO THE SUBWAY STATION ON THE CORNER. AND GO DIRECTLY TO YOUR HOMES. ANYONE WHO DOESN'T WILL GET WHAT THIS FELLOW GOT. ONLY WORSE. I'LL BE PA-

TROLLING THE CITY ALL NIGHT. SO DON'T GET ANY IDEAS. OKAY. START WALKING.''

For a moment they hesitated, leaderless. He lifted the trash can, and hurled it with both hands, with all his remaining strength. It slammed into the brick wall across the street, igniting a shower of sparks; and fell among them, flat as a board.

He cupped his hands to his mouth.

"Now!'' he shouted.

Time dangled painfully, like a hangnail. If they didn't obey, if they moved out through the city according to their plan, mugging, raping, breaking heads, he was through. He might catch a handful, but the rest would get away, would do as they pleased. His weakness would be exposed, for all time to come. Dallas would move forward with its plot, unimpeded. He had retired undefeated. Now, coming back, he would be a laughing-stock.

A disgruntled voice rose from the crowd.

"Elitist pig!''

He looked around, puzzled. What would Porky's mother be doing here?

But it was all over. The edge of the crowd began moving, first slowly, then faster, up the block. Began to funnel into the subway entrance. A defeated army, surrendering without a fight.

He held his breath till the last lingering muggers disappeared. Till the street was empty. Then he stepped down from the wall, onto the roof, and leaned against it, exhausted.

"Mother of Nietzsche,'' he said, quietly. "We did it.''

Peter Pan lay supine on the roof, in the jacket and jeans he had pulled over the uniform. Smiling at the moon.

Brinkley sat cross-legged beside him.

"Thanks, Peter,'' he said.

"Anytime, my man.''

"If there's anything I can do to repay you . . .''

"Forget it,'' Peter said. He sat upright, pulled a joint from his pocket, and lit it. He inhaled, deep.

"I still owe you from the last time. When you taught me to think Good Thoughts."

"You still doin' that shit?" Peter said.

"What do you mean? It helps. Smoother takeoffs."

Peter held out the joint.

"Take a puff of this," he said. "Free fare to Never-Never Land."

"You smoke grass before flying?"

"Every time. Doesn't burn holes in your brain, the way Good Thoughts do."

"I better not," Brinkley said. "I've still got a long night ahead."

"You want me to stick around?"

"No. It won't work twice. From now on it's *super a super*."

They stood, and shook hands.

"What about your uniform?" Peter said.

"Drop it by the hotel in the morning." He paused. "Or keep it as a souvenir . . . in case I don't make it through the night."

Peter squeezed his arm.

"You'll make it," he said.

"You want a cab?"

"Never find one this time of night. Besides, it's a good way to get killed."

Peter puffed on his joint; held his breath; let the smoke out slowly through his nostrils; and began to drift high over the roof, heading west. Waving good-bye.

Brinkley watched Peter disappear gracefully across town.

Then he ducked, too late, as a giant bottle of Coca-Cola fell out of the starry sky, and konked him on the head.

He collapsed to the rooftop, dazed and shaken.

"Hope you d-d-don't mind my d-dropping in," the Coke bottle said.

Brinkley knew, without opening his eyes. It was Elastic Man.

He touched his head. Nothing seemed to be broken. He looked up at the towering bottle.

"Stretch O'Toole?" he said.

He felt like an idiot, talking to soda pop.

"The r-real thing," the Coke bottle said.

Brinkley had heard that about Elastic Man. If his resilience didn't wear you out, his stupid commercials and his terrible puns would.

"You're B-B-Brinkley," the Coke bottle said. The voice came from somewhere around the neck, the words stretched out by stuttering.

Brinkley paled.

"Who told you that?"

"A sweet little c-c-cookie said you was askin' around."

Lorna Doone!

That put a new complexion on the coming battle. It would have to be a fight to the finish. Even if he survived, his secret identity would be in jeopardy—unless Elastic Man died.

He began to perspire. In all his years of heroism, he had never killed a man.

Was this giant bottle in front of him really a man?

"Enough of the p-p-p-pause that r-refreshes," the bottle said. "The b-b-battle is at hand."

With that, the bottle started tipping over, falling on him.

Brinkley leaped back, out of the way; then smashed his fist into the midsection of the Coke bottle. The first real punch he had thrown in eight years.

But the bottle wasn't there. His fist landed without damage in a soft, squishy mess. A soggy bowl of Wheaties.

With a quick flip, the bowl tipped over, and covered him. Brinkley had to shove with all his strength to get out from under.

He kicked at the bowl.

Before his boot landed, the cereal had transformed itself into a Chevrolet. He was kicking the tire.

No one over six will believe this, he thought, forgetting that Elastic Man's best-known trick—falling dominoes—had terrified a nation.

Angrily, he smashed his fist into the windshield. It plowed harmlessly into a four-pack of toilet paper.

"Asshole!" the toilet paper mocked; and wrapped itself around him in a paper embalming.

Brinkley hurled himself off the roof, hoping to crush Elastic Man beneath him; half expecting to wake from a crazy dream; to find that he had hurled himself from his bed onto the floor.

He landed in a huge apple pie.

If this was a dream he was trapped in, it wasn't his.

He slogged his legs through the goo; and thought Good Thoughts, with some difficulty; and leaped to a flagpole that extended out from the second floor of the warehouse.

Elastic Man became the Stars and Stripes, whipping in his face.

He wondered at the meaning of Elastic Man's ballet. Probably it had no meaning at all. Like life. Random acts, without nuances to ponder. Like sex after marriage.

(Still, he hoped Gene Kelly would do it in the movie.)

Suddenly the flag dropped from the pole. And Brinkley heard a scream. It was Peggy, in the street below, where he had left her. Elastic Man had grabbed her in a large, spongy fist.

A tremor like an electric charge coursed through him at the

sight. Peggy screaming, desperate to be saved. Just like the good old days.

He had put up enough of a fight to make it look good. He had to act now. His last resort. His briar-patch gamble: that he had guessed right about how they had weakened him. And that Elastic Man was too low down in the plot to have been told how. The brawn, not the brains.

"Stop!" he yelled.

Elastic Man turned, clutching Peggy in his fist.

"I can't destroy you," Brinkley called down from the flag-pole. "But you can't destroy me, either. Only Cronkite can do that. And the only place there's any Cronkite is out in space. Put the girl down, and we'll call it a draw."

Elastic Man snickered. He extended his arm sixty feet, and wrapped long fingers around Brinkley.

Brinkley squirmed, faking. Elastic Man pulled him off the pole, and began to stride across Manhattan on legs a hundred yards high; Peggy and Brinkley wrapped in his hands like tiny dolls.

Peggy was screaming, her voice thin and childlike.

"Stop bluffing," Brinkley shouted at the nostrils he could see far above him.

A maniacal smile on his face, Elastic Man stopped beside the Empire State Building, and set Peggy down on top of it.

"W-wait here, my p-pet," he said.

"Cut it out," Brinkley taunted. "You can't fly."

Elastic Man grinned again. He stretched his free hand around the top of the building, down to the twin towers of the World Trade Center (scaring the hell out of late diners at the top-floor restaurant), and back. He had transformed his arm into the world's largest slingshot.

He placed Brinkley in the center of it, and began to step back with half-mile strides, till he was standing near the river. His arm, extended across lower Manhattan and back, was taut.

"I'm Stretch," he couldn't resist saying. "F-f-fly me."

"Wait," Brinkley said. "Before you kill me, answer one question. Who's the brains behind this?"

"P-p-p . . ." Elastic Man said.

Brinkley waited, uncertain where to look with his eyes.

"P-P-Peppy."

"Who's that?"

But Elastic Man wasn't listening anymore. The one thing that couldn't stretch was his patience.

Abruptly, he snapped the slingshot that was his arm.

Brinkley was propelled as from a catapult.

He soared into the night sky, higher and higher above the city. Like a Saturn rocket fired into space.

The rushing air was cool against his skin. He kept his arms at his sides, cutting down the resistance. His cape billowed behind him. Higher and higher he soared, till the lights of the city no longer were visible below him.

He passed a doghouse in the sky, trailing smoke. A beagle wearing goggles and a scarf was aboard. The beagle was singing, ". . . Inky Dinky Parlezvous."

Higher and higher he soared. He looked down. The earth was a grapefruit beneath him. Then it disappeared altogether.

Still he traveled on, deeper into space. Exerting no effort. Floating free on Elastic Man's momentum. Growing stronger by the minute. Stronger and stronger as he left behind the civilization made by man, and breathed the pure ozone of space. His natural element.

He had guessed right about how they had done it. They had saturated earthly goods with deadly Cronkite; weakening him by fouling his environment. But here, in deep space, he was becoming his old self!

Higher and higher he soared, far beyond the Earth's gravitational pull. Using some of his own returning power now. His lungs were clearing, his muscles tingling with forgotten strength. He felt himself becoming one with his Creators.

Higher, ever higher. Drifting, streaking. Solar systems passing like telephone poles outside the Swansdown Railroad windows.

Higher still.

Leaving behind the humdrum of daily routine; the commuting; the copy desk; the bills, the boredom; for now at least.

Higher. Ever higher. Knifing through the ether.

He wished his daughters could see him.

Higher still.

His arms were extended over his head, his fists clenched, his left toe straight as an arrow, his right knee bent. His body sleek, his cape flowing gracefully. He was in his old flying form. Familiar everywhere. Soul-stirring (all modesty aside).

It's like riding a bicycle, he thought. You never forget.

Suns, galaxies, black holes drifted by on either side of him. Still he streaked, deeper into space. He rotated his body, floated like a child on water. He had work to do on Earth—he had to get rid of Elastic Man before he revealed his identity—but he allowed himself a few more moments of drifting ecstasy.

He closed his eyes against a thousand suns, floated on soft currents of serenity. Through purple clouds, violet, red, orange, yellow, green, blue. Through a golden door.

He felt as if he had come to rest. He opened his eyes. Pure white light surrounded him, like the inside of a sunlit cloud.

He stood. There was only white mist below his feet; and yet he could walk on it.

He thought he heard voices in the distance. He began to walk toward them through the mist. He came to a doorway hung with curtains of beaded stardust. He parted the curtains, and stepped through.

A world he had never seen spread before him. Fairyland castles. Pure streams winding through green fields. Explosions of flowers in every direction. Silver unicorns grazing orange grass.

Birds filled the skies. Hummingbirds. Bluebirds. Cardinals. And great birds he had never seen before, with large wings flapping slowly, like ceiling fans. Birds that seemed to talk to each other.

People!

He grabbed for support at a signpost beside the narrow gold road on which he was standing. And noticed the silver letters on the sign. They said:

2,873,469,201 FRIENDLY SOULS
WELCOME YOU TO
HEAVEN

His knees went weak. He sat on a yellow rock that seemed to materialize beside him.

Heaven! In all his flying years he had never come here. He felt guilty, as if he were trespassing. He knew he didn't belong. He was still alive.

He looked about. His fondest wish, and it was true. It was not merely worms that awaited, but this. A gold and silver world . . .

"Hello, David."

He was startled by a human voice. Even more startled to hear his own name. He turned. A beautiful young woman was standing beside him, dressed in a white lace gown that reached to the floor. A garland of flowers was in her hair. Above it, a halo glowed.

"I . . . hello . . . I didn't mean to . . . I blundered in here. . . ."

The woman smiled.

"Don't fret," she said. "We allow visitors at times."

"And you're . . . ?"

"Mary."

"Mother of God!" he said.

He fell to his knees, and kissed the woman's hand. She bid him rise.

He was trembling. She noticed it.

"I better go," he said.

"Don't be frightened. You're perfectly safe here. If you like, I'll show you around."

She took his arm, and they began to walk down spotless streets. Heaven reminded him of Seattle.

"You've come at a busy time," she said. "We're preparing for the big celebration."

He felt impertinent merely speaking with her; as if he were walking on sacred eggs. But she seemed relaxed, natural.

"What celebration?" he said, politely.

"Why, the bimillennium, of course. The year 2000. The anniversary of the founding of Heaven. It's less than a quarter-century away. We have lots to do."

His discomfit was increasing. He felt garish in his blue tights, red shorts, purple mask. Everyone else in the streets was wearing white.

"We're expecting millions of tourists," Mary continued. "We'll be throwing the gates open. We have to prepare. Most people can't fly, like yourself. So we're building a stairway to paradise. That takes a lot of souls right there."

"I can imagine," he said. Though he couldn't.

"Then there's refreshment. We'll need lots of little manna and nectar stands. Not to mention rest rooms, which of course we usually don't need at all."

He had no place being here, speaking with her. Everyone else had wings. An irony that was not lost on him.

"I better go," he said.

She pointed to a large gingerbread house on the next block, from which the sound of silver hammering came.

"Souvenirs," she said. "We borrow Santa's workshop during the off-season. There's so much to make. Replicas of the pearly gates, filled with bourbon. Framed portraits of Our Father, done last week by Gilbert Stuart. Ashtrays that say, 'I'll Get to Heaven Before Ya.' Cute, don't you think?"

He realized what was bothering him. Everything about Heaven was cute.

She led him to a window of the workshop. Inside he could see people bent over long tables, the sleeves of their white robes rolled. Among the workers were faces he recognized from his travels back through time. Washington. Rembrandt. Shakespeare. Hieronymous Bosch. (Heaven must have been a jolt for him, Brinkley thought.) And Morris Feinstein. That surprised him most of all.

"Can I go in and talk to them?"

"Sorry," Mary said. "It's against union rules."

He nodded. They moved past the workshop to the Elysian Fields, where souls who had finished work were playing Elys; a game not unlike cricket.

"It's going to be wonderful, the bimillennium," Mary said. "We'll start advertising it on Earth about 1995. In all the better magazines."

She seemed to have a one-track mind.

He became aware of a profound quiet; and realized why.

"There aren't any children up here," he said.

Mary smiled.

"That's why it's called Heaven."

She looked at her sundial.

"I hope we'll meet again," she said. "But for now, your visiting time is over."

She took his arm, and led him down a wide golden boulevard, toward the towering pearly gates.

"You can leave by the front door," she said.

They stopped inside the gates.

"I want to thank you for the tour," Brinkley said. "And also . . ." He didn't know how to phrase it. "And also for your Son. For all the comfort he has brought to . . ."

"My son!" she said. She clutched his arm. "You know about my son?"

"Of course. Everyone knows about your Son. . . ."

Her knees crumbled. The color drained from her face. She fainted.

He caught her in his arms. Feeling . . . holy.

"How do you know?" she whispered, recovering. There was desperation in her voice.

"The Bible. The New Testament. Everyone knows of Jesus."

192

She looked at him. The color flooded back to her face. She started to laugh; and even to blush.

"Jesus?" she said. "Who do you think I am?"

"Mary. You said so. The Virgin Mar . . ."

She was shaking her head; tears of joy flowing down her cheeks.

"I guess I should be flattered," she said. "But I'm not *that* Mary."

"You're not?"

"I thought you knew me. I'm Mary Mantra."

He clapped his hand over his eyes. He felt like an idiot. His face was as red as his shorts.

"In that white dress," he said. "With the halo . . . I'm sorry."

"It's okay," she said, laughing. "No harm done. But if you visit the Captain again, say hello. And tell him to get off his ass and get back to work. Tell him I'm fine up here."

"I will," Brinkley said.

They shook hands.

"Have a good flight back," Mary said.

He left her then, and drifted easily, out through the pearly gates, out into the everlasting blue. When he reached a good height he looked back, to see what the gates looked like from the front. They were shaped like an arch, all bright and sparkly. Ornate gold letters in Gothic print spelled out the Heavenly motto, the oath all souls must take before entering. The letters spelled:

I AM NOT A CROOK

Beneath them, on one leg of the arch, was a smaller, blue and white sign that said Approved by AAA.

Mary was still standing in the gateway, looking petite. Brinkley cupped his hands to his mouth, and called out, "The oath . . . How do you know if someone's lying?"

Her shouted words drifted back musically, as on a pleasant breeze: "It's like at an airport. The gate buzzes."

He waved, and turned, and streaked through the ether, leaving Heaven behind; streaked through the outer galaxies, toward the solar system; toward his unfinished business on the planet Earth.

He reached the edge of Earth's gravitational field, and hovered there. He could not go too close. If he returned to America, to New York, he would be weakened again. He would not be equal to the battle that still awaited. He needed to fight it up here.

His renewed strength left no doubt as to how they had done it. It was all there, in the list of XYZ's holdings. First they had gotten contracts for scientific probes, deep in space. Experiments, they were called, to aid space travel. In reality they were gathering Cronkite—huge meteors from the exploded planet—and bringing them back to Earth.

Then came dissemination. They didn't know who he was, but they knew he was living somewhere as a private citizen. So they bought up all sorts of manufacturing companies, and began introducing tiny traces of Cronkite into the products—into plastics, into building materials, into consumer goods, even into food. The traces were so minute even he couldn't detect them; so infinitesimal that they didn't destroy him. But with each passing year the quantity of Cronkite in the environment built up around him. By now there was probably Cronkite in his toothpaste; in the carpet in the living room; in the polyester dresses the children wore; in the copy paper at the office; in the concrete of all the new buildings in midtown; in Pamela's makeup; in Bernstein's flea powder. There certainly had been a dose of it in the new pipes and plumbing installed in the men's room at the office. It had knocked him out.

Cronkite pervaded the nation now, and most of the civilized world. There was little doubt about that. Wherever he lived, he would be weak—if he returned to Earth.

The most difficult decision of his life loomed ahead.

He pushed it from his mind. He had work to do.

He flipped on his gamma-eye vision, and focused on New York; on the Empire State Building. Only a few seconds, Earth time, had passed since Elastic Man shot him into space. Stretch was still atop the building, clutching Peggy in his fist like some giant ape, peering into space; making sure Brinkley was gone forever.

He needed a Top-Three brainstorm. How to save Peggy, and destroy Elastic Man, without returning to Earth?

A small object bumped against his foot. He looked down. It was a communications satellite, in orbit around the Earth. He had hardly noticed, but space was full of them—American and Russian satellites, some still functioning, others long since burned out.

Just what he needed! Heaven-sent.

He picked up the satellite, and was about to pull it apart, when a voice began crackling through it. He listened.

"This is Marilyn Berger reporting via satellite from Moscow. Soviet foreign minister Werner von Oskar was arrested at his suburban *dacha* early this morning by the Russian secret police. According to the Soviet news agency Tass, von Oskar was accused of being a spy in the pay of an American right-wing organization. The foreign minister, Tass said, was involved in a complex plot to destroy an unnamed but prominent American superhero. The arrest thwarted what Tass called a 'worldwide fascist coup.' According to unofficial sources, the Kremlin received incriminating information about von Oskar early today in a hotline phone call from President James L. Keith to Soviet party leader Leonid Pirogin. No further information is available at this time.''

The voice faded into static. ''An unnamed but prominent American superhero,'' Brinkley repeated. He smiled wanly. A hollow legacy.

He replaced the crackling satellite in its orbit, and found a dead one nearby. Using his superstrength, he refashioned the parts, and put them together in a new form. Then he flew lower, carefully; positioning himself at the proper angle, amid maximum electromagnetic radiation.

He was glad he had majored in science.

He focused the laser he had made. It was still night in New York, but suddenly the most powerful beam ever seen cut through the dark, and illuminated with a burning hot spotlight the top of the Empire State Building.

Elastic Man screamed as the piercing sliver of light passed through him.

Brinkley tilted the laser, cutting the beam back and forth across Elastic Man's body. With his superhearing he could hear Peggy sobbing with terror in Elastic Man's outstretched arm; Elastic Man howling with pain as the laser burned through him; as slowly, inexorably, his elastic body began to melt.

The screams tore into Brinkley's conscience. But there was no other way to save Peggy. No other way to be rid of Elastic Man.

He forced himself to hold the laser in place. He could see Elastic Man's flesh loosening, running in a sticky goo down the sides of the building; an ice cream cone in summer.

Carefully he kept the beam away from Peggy. But as Elastic Man weakened, his arm collapsed to his side.

Peggy screamed. A blood-thinning scream.

And fell from the top of the Empire State Building, toward the pavement a hundred and two stories below.

Brinkley was ready. He dropped the handmade laser, and swooped slightly closer to Earth. With his superbreath he blew a ferocious downdraft into Thirty-fourth Street. The draft filled the street, and rebounded upward. Peggy's green Diane von Furstenberg dress billowed in the breeze, like a parachute; and slowed her descent.

Ever so slowly she drifted downward on the soft cushion of air. The street was crowded with National Guardsmen who had rushed to the scene when they heard the screams. They were all looking up at her descending form; and cheering wildly.

Brinkley was surprised at the cheers. He was much too high up to be seen. He flipped on his gamma-eye vision, to see what they were cheering about.

"Creeping Cronkite!" he said.

She wasn't wearing any panties.

"Creeping Cron . . ." he began again; and crashed into the smoking doghouse that was still careening crazily through the sky.

"Merde!" the goggled beagle said.

"Woof yourself," Brinkley replied.

He didn't wait for an answer, but moved out of the way and let the doghouse pass.

He focused his supersight again. Elastic Man was gone; nothing left of him but a puddle of goo atop the Empire State Building. Peggy was in the arms of the guardsmen. They were still cheering.

Brinkley looked away. He felt curiously unsatisfied; almost depressed. His first battle—his first triumph—in eight years, felt empty; anticlimactic. As if violence wasn't his thing anymore.

A mid-superlife crisis?

He felt panicky. To what would he devote the rest of his life, if not law, order and mayhem? What good is superstrength if the thrill is gone?

As if in answer to his unspoken question, a bright burning corona appeared beside him. A gray-haired woman stepped out of it, dressed in a tattered pink tutu, carrying a silver wand. Perched precariously on her head, slipping to one side, was a gem-studded tiara. Several of the gems were missing.

"Who are you?" Brinkley said.

He was still upset about the mistake with Mary. He didn't

want to do it again. It had been a problem all his life. He couldn't remember faces.

"I'm the fairy godmother," the old woman said. "I'm here to make any wish come true."

Brinkley was suspicious.

"Whose fairy godmother?" he said. "I don't have a fairy godmother."

"What does it matter whose?" the fairy godmother said. "Don't look a gift wish in the mouth."

She sounded crochety.

"Sorry," Brinkley said. "I don't talk to strange fairy godmothers. They can be big trouble."

"Creepo," the fairy godmother said. "Everyone's so suspicious these days. Pop into a bedroom at midnight, and you get a faceful of Mace. It ain't easy anymore being supernatural. I thought you at least would understand."

"Well . . ." Brinkley said, beginning to relent.

"No, don't apologize," the fairy godmother said. "I'll tell you, if it'll make ya feel better. I'm Cinderella's fairy godmother."

"Cinderella's?"

He was impressed.

"Then why are you offering *me* a wish?"

"I don't know myself," the fairy godmother said. "I was just passing by. You sure looked like you needed one. Call it a good deed."

"But what about Cinderella? I wouldn't want to use up one of hers."

"That slut?" the fairy godmother said. "Fuck her. She doesn't need me anymore. Kicked me out of the palace."

"Cinderella? I don't believe it."

"Yeah. You wouldn't recognize her. Liberated, that's what she calls it. Kicked the prince out of her life, too. But kept the palace, of course. Sleeps with anything in pants. Mice, pumpkins, anything. Doesn't want my help anymore, she said. Doesn't need me. She'll make it on her own. I'm too judgmental, she said. Trying to keep her in her place. Is that gratitude?"

Brinkley was reluctant to commit himself. You never knew what conversation was being taped.

"That's too bad," he said.

"Yeah, well, that's supernatural life for ya. Listen, I ain't got much time. You wanna wish, or dontcha?"

"I don't know," Brinkley said. "Let me think. . . ."

He could wish for a son. Or to have all the Cronkite on Earth evaporate. Or . . .

There was no time to ponder. An eerie dark form was streaking toward him from Earth; a figure clad all in black, with a flash of yellow lightning on the chest; the head covered with a black hood; like an executioner of old.

Brinkley recognized him at once; had, in fact, been expecting him. His forehead broke out in sweat. His knees began to quiver.

It was the dread Prince of Darkness.

The Scourge of Evil.

The bane of Poughkeepsie.

Despised despoiler of Peggy's virginity.

Demoniac!

And he looked like he meant business.

"I know my wish," Brinkley blurted.

There was no response.

He looked around for the fairy godmother.

She was gone.

"F. Lee Bulldoody!" Brinkley said.

He fled. He streaked away from the pull of Earth, across the solar system; Demoniac in swift pursuit.

He looked back. Demoniac was gaining.

They had never met before. Brinkley had to test him; find out if he was as fast and tough and strong as his reputation. Even if it hurt.

He sped toward Saturn, flipped around a ring, and took off in another direction. The maneuver surprised Demoniac. Brinkley put more distance between them.

Strong, but not too bright. That was the book on Demoniac.

Beyond the solar system Brinkley flew, past Taurus the bull, past Aries the ram, past Leo the manager. Demoniac gained ground in the open spaces. Just as Brinkley had heard, evil could outdistance good every time.

In a few seconds Demoniac would catch him. Brinkley slipped into a black hole, left by a long-gone star, and hid in the absence of light; as in a cosmic closet.

It was a mistake. The Prince of Darkness could see without light. He ate stars for breakfast. He had invented black holes. He followed Brinkley into the tar-black void. Brinkley could hear his doglike breath; but he couldn't see him.

A single, terrible word bellowed out of the darkness; the one dread word feared throughout the universe: "Bugga-bugga!"

A microsecond later a fist like God's sledge hammer crashed into Brinkley's jaw.

The punch sent him spinning, head over heels, out of the black hole. For a moment he thought his superjaw was broken.

Demoniac was upon him before the shock wore off, landing a solid punch in his stomach.

"Maybe we should play chess instead," Brinkley said, with a gasp.

Demoniac's reply was muffled by his black hood. Something about not understanding chess but how about Old Maid.

Brinkley shook off the pain and leaped at Demoniac, landing a solid right to the cheek.

"That one's for Peggy!" he grunted. "Old Maid indeed!"

"Peggy who?" Demoniac said. And whirled and landed a swift kick on Brinkley's Adam's apple.

He feared he would black out from the pain. Instinctively he sped away, as if on automatic pilot; past Libra; past Virgo; past Aquarius (which looked surprisingly like Norman Taylor).

He braked suddenly, turned, and slammed his fist into the Evil One's chin. Demoniac stopped like a truck hitting a wall; then churned forward again, driven by some boiling volcano inside him; some childhood trauma, perhaps.

They squared off, toe to toe, slugging each other with superpowerful blows. Stars circled their heads; some real, some not. First one, then the other, flew off for a breather, then came forward again.

Hour after hour the battle raged, beyond the most distant constellations, deep into the outer reaches of space. The battle of the century; with no home TV. Neither could conquer the other.

But Demoniac was younger, and by the sixth hour Brinkley felt himself growing short of breath; felt his superlimbs beginning to weaken. He started to hallucinate. He imagined a television screen, with a face on it saying, "I'm Demoniac. But people don't recognize me without my hood. So I always carry an American Express credit card."

If the battle lasted much longer, he would be finished.

He sped away for a rest. Without realizing it, he crossed a warning track. He could go no farther. A thin transparent wall, like an embryonic sac, blocked his path.

He was puzzled. He didn't know where he was. Then with a horrid illumination, he realized. He was at the end of the world. The end of the universe. The place he had always meant to visit, on a pleasure trip. The place where space ends.

He whirled. Demoniac was upon him like a bat out of hell (which some people say he is). A thundering punch crashed into his jaw. He tumbled backward, out of control. And fell through the invisible wall at the edge of space.

Into darkness.

Into silence.

Into nothingness.

He trembled with fear. A fear that he had never felt before.

He waited for Demoniac to follow. Nobody came. It was not a place into which one ventured voluntarily. Not even Demoniac.

All strength was gone from his muscles. He felt his will-power leaking from his brain. He drifted, helpless, in the nothingness.

Gradually, without trying, he began to distinguish vague shapes in the negative space around him; sickly, pale-green mists, like jaundiced fog. Shapes without shape, forms without form. Beings of nonbeing. Mists of unshed tears.

He watched them float by, without intent, without direction. Not knowing what they were. And then, with a strange intelligence, like Adam naming the animals, he knew. He recognized them. The pleasure trips he had never taken. The times he wanted to make love and didn't wake her up. The fat pitches he didn't swing at. The fears that putrified friendships. The books he hadn't read (*Little Lulu*, for one). The music he never really listened to, too lost in his own not-so-super thoughts. The love he never consummated with Peggy—it was there, now, drifting by. Out of reach.

All the missed opportunities. That's what filled the place beyond space. The chances not taken. The dances not danced.

The tintinnabulation of the bells of Copenhagen, never heard by toilers in New York. The screams not screamed, the curses not cursed, the hands never held, the whispers never spoken. All of them palpable, still existing, here in this place beyond recovery. If Phoebe was still alive—if they were still on good terms—then Holden ought to tell her, if she doesn't know already. This is the place the ducks go in the winter.

He tried to close his eyes against them. The languages unlearned. The birdsongs never heard. The expense accounts not cheated on.

He could not even blink.

He tried to be cynical; to picture himself as Scrooge, watching the past go by in a maudlin morality play. It didn't work. He was caught in a choke of emotion.

The mists became a parade of human shapes—farmers, businessmen, soldiers . . . people in every occupation imaginable. He was puzzled at first. But then, again, he knew. They were secret identities. All the secret identities never revealed, never attempted—only dreamed. The rural life for the city man who never broke away. The season on the pro golf tour the insurance man putted away in his office, into ashtrays. The night watchman leading the Lord's Prayer. The time salesman's dreamlife as a pitcher. All the secret identities into which life was never breathed; all of them unsouls, floating in perpetuity now in the place beyond space. Beyond the rim of the universe.

All the unbeings we dared not be.

He was shaken; determined to leave this place, if it was at all possible. Gathering every last ounce of superwill, of superstrength, he flew as if in slow motion back toward the invisible wall; struggling; groping; pushing his way through the limbo mists; till he reached the tear in the sac through which he had fallen, like SuperAlice.

There he paused. He was desperately weak from negative space. And Demoniac might still be beyond the wall, waiting.

The time had come.

To roll the universe into a ball.

Prayerfully.

Slowly, he took off his mask. Unfastened his cape. Pulled off his boots; his shorts; his jersey with the weird emblem; stuffed them all into the pocket of the cape; rolled up the cape; shoved it under his arm.

He stood revealed now in the outfit Max had given him, eons ago; that very afternoon.

He breathed deeply, his very life at stake. He pulled himself onto the transparent wall, straining; barely able to keep his grasp; and dove through the tear, like a diver heedless of the ice water waiting below.

Demoniac whirled to face him.

A short, sharp gasp escaped from beneath the black hood. Like a fart.

"Captain Mantra!"

And a fierce fork of lightning split the darkness.

At this point, dear reader, it is necessary to backtrack, briefly, in time; to uncloak the deadliest, best-kept secret of the superworld of heroes and villains, the skeleton in the supercloset: the fateful origins of Demoniac, Prince of Evil.

(This chapter is not for children.)

It happened one fine spring evening many years ago. Billy and Mary Button were on their way home from the blue-collar factory where they worked, making blue collars. Suddenly they were grabbed from behind by henchmen of their archenemy, Dr. Piranha Spock. Gags were pulled tight across their mouths before they could say their secret word—tomato-herring—and be transformed by lightning into Captain and Mary Mantra, indomitable foes of injustice.

They were dragged without ceremony—not even a little incense—into an abandoned warehouse, where they were stripped naked, bound hand and foot, and left in a windowless steel cell. Calmly they looked about for some protruding corner or molding on which to rip off their gags. But there were none. The walls, the floor, the ceiling, were smooth as a baby's tushy.

Set high in one wall, near the ceiling, was a television screen. It clicked on, and a face appeared; the hated face of Dr. Spock.

"Hello, my children," Dr. Spock said. "I want to welcome

you . . . to your deaths. Even as I speak, the walls of your cell are beginning to close in on you; to crush you to death. That will be the end of the Mantras. Nothing can save you now. Not even TM.''

Without another word, his face clicked off. It was replaced on the screen by a rerun of "I Love Lucy."

The steel walls began to close in from all sides. Billy and Mary squirmed frantically, trying to loosen their gags, so they could say tomato-herring. But with no luck.

They tried to rub off their gags on each other's bodies. It didn't work. Instead, rubbing against each other stark naked, they began to get excited. Billy became erect. Mary grew goggle-eyed at the pulsing sight; a busty Orphan Annie. Fluids secreted inside her.

The walls pressed tight against their backs. They were caught in a jumble of emotions: brother–sister love, sexual excitement, the fear of approaching death.

Their faces came together, to kiss good-bye through their gags. Mary's thighs opened. In the face of death any sense of sin between them washed away. Their long-repressed desire gushed forth. Their loins pressed together. Mary took Billy inside her, lovingly; desperately.

Ethel and Fred Mertz giggled on the screen.

Billy and Mary began to rock in rhythm. The walls pressed tighter. Their lips twisted frantically as they bit at each other in their passion.

Their frenzied mouths tore through each other's gags.

Instinctively, at the precise moment of orgasm, they said tomato-herring. Lightning streaked down out of the Heavens, splitting the steel cell. Billy and Mary Button, their genitals locked in ecstasy, were transformed in mid-coitus into Captain and Mary Mantra.

Their fluids poured forth, commingled; fused by the lightning.

At that moment the giant fuckmeter on Uranus, which registers the degree of perfection of every sex act in the universe, registered a 999.7—the highest score ever recorded.

It eclipsed by five full points the old record of 994.7, set by
Tiny Tim and Miss Vicki on their wedding night.

(Leda and the Swan had a 996.1, but with an asterisk.)

At monitoring stations throughout the galaxies, spontaneous
applause burst forth. It was the first original sin since Adam.

When Captain and Mary Mantra pulled apart, they were no
longer in danger. The steel walls buckled against their super
bodies. They flew off to Harvard in search of Dr. Spock.

Their lives returned to normal soon after. They never spoke
of what had happened in the steel room. But a few months later,
Mary Button discovered that she was pregnant.

Abortion was not legal in those days, so she left the blue-
collar factory, and went to the Tough Nookie Home for Unwed
Mothers, in upstate New York. She gave the child for adoption
to the Newses, Dick and Jane. They named him Frederick.

To all appearances, Fred was a normal child, until at age
three he was thrown by a horse called National Velvet at the
News farm near Poughkeepsie, and developed a permanent
limp. (National Velvet was mysteriously shot soon after.)

Years later, at his high school graduation, young Fred News
saw the principal, Mr. Conklin, talking with the day's guest
speaker. Delighted, Fred blurted out the speaker's name: "Captain Mantra!"

A streak of forked lightning split the sky. And Fred News
was transformed, by the mention of his true father's name, into
Demoniac, Prince of Darkness.

Beneath his blue satin graduation gown, his white shirt and
red tie had become a black uniform, with yellow lightning on
the chest.

Fred was surprised. And thrilled. What a graduation present
for a boy!

He left the farm the next day, and moved to the big city;
where the black hood he had decided to wear with his uniform
would not be commented on.

He was not qualified for a good job—he had majored in
shop—so he began selling newspapers to support himself. But
his main interest was his hobby. Each night, he would speak his

incestuous father's name, and be transformed into Demoniac, Scourge of Evil. And he would hang out in singles bars. Till morning; when he would speak his father's name once more, and become mortal again.

Before long he had written his own dark legend in the annals of villainy (located, like all annals, in the basement of the Forty-second Street library).

Rumor gradually spread throughout the superworld about Demoniac's origins. But his mortal identity was not widely known, beyond the fact that he was crippled.

So it was, dear reader, that when Brinkley, visiting Heaven, congratulated the wrong Mary about her son, she fainted. (As for what Mary Mantra was doing in Heaven, having committed incest—that is a theological question best left to the priests.)

So it was, too, that when Brinkley heard a crippled youth was involved in the plot against him, he guessed that it might be Demoniac. (Hardly one of his Top-Three hunches.) And when Max Givenchy produced an unclaimed uniform of Captain Mantra's, Brinkley put it on under his own—just in case.

Now let us return to the present.

Brinkley, dressed as Captain Mantra, climbed back through the tear in the invisible wall; staking his life on a gamble.

Demoniac whirled to face him.

A short, sharp gasp escaped from beneath the black hood. Like a fart.

"Captain Mantra!"

A fierce fork of lightning split the darkness.

And transformed Demoniac to his mortal identity. To crippled newsboy Freddie News.

Quickly he tried to say the words again. (He even tried to say tomato-herring; which would not have done any good.) But there was no way. In the pressure of deep space his lungs had collapsed instantly. He could get no breath to speak.

In a matter of seconds his internal organs had imploded. (We told you this wasn't for children.)

He was dead.

With mixed feelings of relief and horror, Brinkley watched

the body of Freddie News drift in a lazy orbit, just inside the wall at the edge of space.

Floating in a similar orbit, a few feet behind him, was his crutch.

Freddie News. Brinkley couldn't get over it. He thought: when you work in a big office building, you never really get to know the other people.

The body drifted away, the crutch following about ten feet behind it like a faithful dog. That's two hundred and fifty dollars I'll never have to pay, Brinkley thought; and felt unworthy, and shoved the thought away.

With the physical battle won, he collapsed against the invisible wall, and rested. Time passed, but there was no way to reckon it. At the place where space ends, time and space become one. His Mickey Mouse watch read zero; and John Cameron Swayze be damned. There was no past, and no future.

It is a time that occurs on Earth only to the blessed.

As his strength returned, he peeled off the Captain Mantra suit, and let it drift away in the dead wake of Freddie News.

"The sins of the fathers . . ." he mumbled, in the awesome emptiness.

He became conscious of his nakedness; and felt, here at the ceiling of the world, like a refugee from the Sistine Chapel. He imagined a headline in the *National Enquirer:* "Astronomer Snaps Space Streaker." He unrolled his uniform and put it on; wondering if this was the last time he would be doing that.

He peered at the invisible wall. The rent through which he had fallen had vanished. The wall was whole again. Rent-free. It seemed to have the capacity to repair itself, like living flesh.

He thought: this wall . . . this invisible separation between ourselves and abandoned dreams . . . could this be the existential center of the universe? The unreal green mists on one side as palpable as the solid flesh on the other?

Metaphysics was not his field. He shrugged, and thought Good Thoughts, and took off toward the stratosphere.

(The stratosphere was named after Karl Xerox Strato, the first superhero, who lived in prehistoric times. It is believed by fundamentalists that Strato's body dissolved into the cosmos after he was slain by Morris Feinstein; and that when other superheroes die, they are reunited with Strato. Brinkley was not certain if this was divine truth or horse manure.)

Moving easily, he flew past the outer galaxies; past the inner galaxies; into the solar system. He knew exactly where he was going. He had a call to make.

He positioned himself at the precise point where Earth was in conjunction with the Sun. The syzygy. He turned, and faced the galactic equivalent of East: the constellation Pyxis.

He felt at ease. He had been here before.

He tried to think of something clever to say. He couldn't. Instead, he bellowed a single word, eight years of anger stored up in it.

"PXYZSYZYGY!"

A cloud of yellow vapor formed in front of him. Out of it, with the suction sound of a plunger, popped a dapper elf, wearing a violet bowler, and carrying a gold walking stick. He was frowning with annoyance.

"You!" the elf said.

"You were expecting Amelia Earhart?"

"She's here already. Has been for years. But you . . . you're thupposed to be dead by now."

"Supposed," Brinkley said. "That's a big word for a midget."

"Elf," Pxyzsyzygy said. "I'm a full-grown elf, not a midget."

"Is that all you have to say?"

The elf had no choice. He conceded defeat.

"Curses," he said. "Foiled again."

"There," Brinkley said, as if speaking to a child. "Doesn't that make you feel better?"

"Rats. If those two idiots had fought you on Earth, you'd be dead."

"Maybe," Brinkley said. "They're not too bright, are they? What do you call them, the Plumbers?"

"No need to get nasty," the elf said.

"Heaven forbid! Just because you tried to kill me . . . tried to take over Earth . . ."

"Good clean fun," Pxyzsyzygy said, twirling his walking stick. "It gets boring out here in thpace. When I visit Earth I need to liven things up. I only get down there once in four years, you know."

"That what you call livening things up? The Kennedys, King, Wallace . . ."

"That wasn't me," the elf said, modestly. "Not personally. Now if you mentioned Thuperman's accident, or Batman's, or the Marvels . . ."

"And I was next," Brinkley said.

"Alas, yes. Who else is there? But tell me. How did you know it was me?"

"Come come, Pxyzsyzygy. Your ego. You can't resist signing your masterpieces, can you? Peppy. P. P. Powell Pugh. I must admit I was slow on the uptake. Slow to put the P before XYZ Industries. But you did want everyone to know. You always do."

The elf's yellow face blushed to orange.

"It's all over now," Brinkley said. "I've spoken your name at the syzygy. You can't return for another four years. Earth is safe from takeover."

"Is it?"

"What do you mean?"

"Open your eyes," Pxyzsyzygy said. "Powell Pugh. Sure, that was my little game. The recluse billionaire. The ultimate capitalist. But where do you think I got the idea? It was a cartoon drawn from life. Look around down on Earth. The big industrialists, the huge corporations. You think they're not already halfway toward where I was heading? Who's going to thtop them from going the rest of the way? You?''

The elf was beginning to sound like Captain Mantra.

"Maybe," Brinkley said.

"Think again. You return to Earth and you're finished as a thuperhero. The place is thaturated with Cronkite. With more being poured into the environment every day, in half the factories in the land. You can't go home again. Haven't you realized that? You've got to thtay out here in thpace, like me. Do your thuper work on thom other planet, if you like. But not on Earth. It might as well not exist for you anymore. Go back there and you're doomed.''

Brinkley said nothing. He had been trying not to think about that. He knew it was true.

The elf tilted his bowler, rakishly, with his walking stick.

"Why, Pxyzsyzygy? You used to be happy with pranks. With mischief. The Cosmic Trickster, that's your role. Why all this? Murder, intrigue . . . ?''

With his name spoken so often, the elf was beginning to fade back into a vapor. All that was left was a yellow half-moon grin, like the smiles ignorant people wear on their lapels to say "Have a nice day"—not realizing whose image they are wearing.

"Cosmic Trickster, shit," the smile said. "I'm tired of playing the clown. Call it Fool's Lib. From now on there will be death, destruction, disease. Maybe even vermin, or frogs. I am God, and I will be worshiped as Him. I *am* worshiped as Him.''

"Not on Earth you're not.''

"Give them time," the smile said. "Give them time.''

The smile was gone. Brinkley was alone in space. More alone than he had ever been.

He looked down at Earth, glowing like a blue-green marble far below him. The familiar emerald and turquoise swirls were as inviting as a freshly made bed. He wanted nothing more than to return there; his home. To sleep a good, long sleep; without dreams.

Tears began to well behind his eyes. It was not fitting for a superman to cry. But there it was. The planet Earth below a blue-green dollop of poison, infested with Cronkite; for which there was no antidote. If he returned there, it was unlikely he could ever again escape its atmosphere. He would be weak, barely able to fly. And would grow weaker day by day, month by month; until in a year, or five, or ten—there was no way to say exactly—he would die.

He pulled off his mask, to wipe away tears that had filtered beneath it. And put it on again. Pamela was there on Earth; and Allison; and Jennifer. Perhaps even a new baby now. Would he ever see it? And how could he explain?

Earth was his home, the only home he had known. Chosen for him by his parents, Archie and Edith, in the last days of Cronk. Chosen not even by them, but by higher powers; by the Lord Gods Nietzsche and Namath, who guided their hand. He

217

had come to feel almost more Earthling than Cronker; albeit a bit special.

And now?

The choices were spread before him, invitingly, like the spread legs of beauties; out there, in the distant galaxies. The six other planets that harbored human life. He could take up residence on any of them, and resume his role as a superhero, unhindered by Cronkite, cheered and honored by the populace. He could start a new life, a new family. He could live through eternity, never aging, doing his good works.

He could go to the planet Nudj, land of the long-stemmed rain. Or Bazoom, where strange myths grew on trees. Or Wop, or Kike, or Nigger, or Elvis.

Or he didn't have to commit himself to any one. He could travel among them, stopping now here, now there—an itinerant hero, beloved throughout the universe. A girl in every port. It wouldn't be a bad life. Battling monsters, subduing criminals— the life he had been created for. Maybe he would take up the guitar.

There was no other choice. That's what he must do.

And yet, down on Earth, there was Pamela. Allison. Jennifer.

They were his. They needed him.

It's not so, he told himself. Suppose he had died during this long night of combat? Life would go on for them. Pamela would marry again. The children would grow, would become independent. It might even be better for them.

. . . While far out in the universe, their father would become a legend, his name synonymous with all that is good and brave and true. . . .

There was no other choice. Here from the perspective of the cosmos he could face without flinching the accumulated sadness of his recent life on Earth. The times each day when there would be a weight in his chest that would move up back of his eyes, until he wanted to lie down in private and cry himself to sleep, for no reason at all. That was the hell of it. For no reason at all. He would look around and see a refrigerator bulging with food, a wife he loved who loved him in return, two little girls growing up bright and true, a job he could keep for the rest of his life if he wanted, that would take care of all the bills—he would see all this and still he would want to cry; would awaken in the middle of the night sometimes and stare at the ceiling in the dark, at the ghostly circle of light cast by a street lamp, and he would recall the world-saving exploits of his youth as if they had been performed by a stranger. He knew he could not come close to performing them now, and would question whether he ever really had. Either way his wish would be the same. He would wish he could fall asleep again and never awaken.

Each time, of course, he would not fall asleep till the gray of dawn burned out the lamplit circle. Then he would be awakened by Pamela and the children stirring. Light would be knifing in beneath the shade, or a new winter snow would be falling, and his despair of the dark night would burrow deep beyond reach into his soul, whitewashed over by the mechanics of the day—till without warning in midafternoon at work it would peep out again like a gopher, and he would walk to the water fountain or down the hall until it passed.

Each time he would review the litany of his blessings. And each time the same answer screamed inside him: It was not enough.

But he didn't know what would be enough. What would satisfy him. What would fill the emptiness.

He had no complaints. Except . . . everything.

Sometimes he thought they should move from Middleville. He should quit his job, and they should go to Savannah, or Missoula, or Santa Fe. Someplace with a pretty name and a pretty view, where the beauty of nature would swallow up human grief, and paint it o'er with unity, oneness, peace.

Other times he knew it would do no good. He was a Cronker amid Earthlings, and always would be. No one would ever know him. He would never know another person. He was an alien, alone in the universe. It was his fate. Cursing it made his fate neither better nor worse.

Now that he knew the cause of his physical weakness—the

spread of Cronkite through the arteries of civilization—he knew that moving to another town, another country, would make little real difference. Cronkite was everywhere. The days when he could ever again have a sense of mission . . . down there . . . were gone.

And yet he was not streaking away from Earth, away into the stratosphere, into a new superlife. He was hovering in place; looking down at the emerald-turquoise swirls; wistfully.

He felt like a balloon, flying high, but still held down by a string; an umbilical cord; a cord he would have to cut.

The cord of love.

Above waited a physical—even a spiritual—rebirth. A challenging new career. A full new life.

Below was his family. Three human beings. Perhaps, at this moment, four.

He remembered a small incident from a picnic the previous summer. They had gone to Mystic Seaport to see the old sailing ships, and afterward he had tumbled in the grass with the girls while Pamela grilled hamburgers. An orange-breasted robin hopped near them, and then lit out for a distant treetop. Jennifer, her small arms draped loosely around his neck, had said, "Daddy, wouldn't it be nice to fly like a bird?" He had replied that he imagined it would be very nice indeed. But that if people could fly, then birds would no longer be special.

He hadn't thought the answer would satisfy her; but it had.

Now, alone in space, hovering, he found himself waiting for a similar answer himself. Some sign. Some revelation. Knowing there would be none.

Finally, unable to hover in place any longer, he shed his paralysis with a wrenching motion. He kicked his legs, like a swimmer; and filled his lungs with the pure heady ozone of free will.

He thought Good Thoughts; a ritual; as if crossing himself.

And soared off into space.

Toward the North Star he streaked; and circled it, and continued on beyond. Through the Milky Way; out toward the scattered stars of the distant galaxies, twinkling pure silver in the blue of eternity.

He passed the golden door, through which he had blundered earlier. And continued soaring outward; till he neared the invisible wall.

He paused there, looking down, the entire universe spread before him, gems in a blue-gold setting, exquisite, perfect; creation of the Original Jeweler, the Master Craftsman who had preceded all the others; whom subsequent gods had not been able to match.

He filled himself with the beauty of it all, like a parched wanderer prone beside a stream. The symmetry, the precision. His blood felt purified, his limbs invigorated. The exhaustion of the night's battles had vanished. He felt as powerful as he had ever been.

He switched on his supersight. He scanned the distant universe, until his eyes picked out the tiny blue-green marble, adrift like all the others, yellow, or brown, or red; planets of every color.

Even now he smiled at the sight of it.

Slowly, he flew to the left. To the place in space where Cronk had once been. It was a vacuum now. A black hole. He hovered there, solemn. As if he were visiting a grave. For one last time.

Then he flew on, without tears.

Down and down he flew; his eyes not roaming now; looking neither left nor right; determined not to see the myriad suns, the stars, rushing by. His eyes fixed, unwavering, on his destination. On the blue-green marble growing ever larger below him.

Weakness entered his body like a foreign agent as he descended toward the surface of Earth. Weakness that henceforth would be his life's blood.

He picked out the city and glided toward it, pulled by a gravity that he never again would escape. The gray of approaching dawn outlined the famous skyline, the Empire State Building, the Twin Towers, the RCA Building, the Chrysler Building; bars of a mortal prison to which he was sentencing himself. Prisoner number one on Death Row.

Weariness like lead weights cramped his arms, his legs. Now that he knew that Cronkite was all around him he could almost feel it, a magnet drawing him down, fatal, inexorable.

He had no one to blame but himself. It was his choice.

He picked out the hotel amid the cluster of midtown buildings, and hovered near it with difficulty, fighting fatigue that was making him light-headed. He counted off the floors and the windows, and pulled open the window to his room, and climbed in. The sight of the bed drained the last ounce of his strength. He fell upon it, without even removing his uniform or his mask; and dropped into a deep, weary sleep.

Outside, dawn flared full over the city. Then morning.

How long he had been sleeping before they appeared he had no way to tell. It might have been an hour, or two, or three.

Suddenly they were standing there, beside the bed, looking down at him. Peggy. Punch. Pamela. And the children.

"Hello, Pook," Pamela said.

"Huh? What?"

How did she know it was him? He was wearing his uniform. And his mask.

He looked from one face to the next. All were smiling.

"Hello, Daddy," Allison and Jennifer said together.

"Hello, David," Peggy said.

"Welcome back," Punch said. "How was it?"

He didn't know what to say. His life was swimming before him. Drowning in confusion.

"What . . . how . . . when did you find out?"

"That you were him?" Pamela said.

He nodded.

"You didn't really believe we didn't know," Peggy said.

He could only nod again, dumbly.

"You must think we're pretty stupid," Punch said. "For twenty years you've been going out on assignments, and disappearing—leaving Peggy to cover for you. Why do you think you weren't fired years ago? Of course we knew."

"The first few times, I thought it could be coincidence," Peggy said. "You disappearing just before he showed up. But time after time after time? Really, David."

He couldn't believe this. All these years . . . his masquerade . . . had it all been unnecessary?

He looked at Pamela.

"And you?"

"I'm your wife."

"But . . . you must have hated me. All the deceptions."

"You had to do it. Besides, I knew, so they weren't deceptions."

"You knew from the beginning?"

"Of course."

"But how?"

"A dozen ways. Who else has blue hair?"

224

"You must have despised me when I lost my strength."

She leaned over, and kissed his forehead.

"I love you," she said. "Isn't that enough?"

"Daddy, Daddy," Jennifer said. "Tell us how you beat up Demoniac."

He reached out his arms to the girls, to hug them to him; to hold them tight.

The sound of a key in the door woke him from his dream.

He lay still, perspiring; regaining his bearings. He must have climbed into Peggy's room by mistake.

He heard the door open. He kept his eyes closed. She would want to interview him; to ask him where he had been the past eight years. She would have a million questions. He was not up to that now. He pretended he was still asleep.

He heard her pause, as if surprised by his presence in her room; and then close the door quietly, and tiptoe to the bed; and stand beside it; and place something—her handbag?—on the other bed. He felt her lips touch his forehead lightly, and then her weight on the bed as she sat beside him.

He continued to breathe evenly, waiting for her to leave, or to stretch out on the other bed after her long night at the office. She didn't. Instead he felt her hands at his waist, opening his belt.

To make him more comfortable?

The belt came loose. He felt her slim fingers slip inside his waistband, and caress his belly; and swoop lower, to his root. He inhaled sharply; and then exhaled; resuming the even rhythm.

His mind raced. He would not move. He would remain passive, and see what she would do.

He felt her hand at the base of him, pressing, gently. The blood was rushing, he could feel himself stiffen.

He felt her hand slip out. They were at his hips now, pulling his uniform down. Cool air brushed his crotch. He was exposed.

Both hands were on him now, tickling his balls; caressing,

stroking the upright totem he had become; rubbing his ridges, touching the sides of him as he thickened, his uniform notwithstanding.

The bed creaked as he felt her change position. A new, warm sensation enveloped him. At first he couldn't be sure; but then he knew. Her lips. They were wrapped around him, sucking, ingesting. Pulling at his ridges and then taking him deep against her palate, and then out again. Popping loose in the cool air, feeling her tongue along the sides of him, down under his balls, then up, slipping him into her mouth with a soft sliding squish. The pressure was building, building as he let it all happen, Peggy his first love taking him in her mouth, filling now with his rigid flesh her ache of twenty years. How could he deny her?

He felt her soft, warm mouth sliding over him, pulling, urging, insistent, until he could hold back no longer, and exploded into her mouth, or shoulder, or hair, he knew not which.

He lay still, exhausted, content, his eyes closed; feeling the weight of her head against his belly. Pamela would have to forgive him, he had not sought this, had barely even participated; it was not even him, Brinkley; it was the uniform, was all.

Still, there was a tender feeling.

He reached his hand down, gently, to touch her hair.

And opened his eyes, startled.

It wasn't Peggy.

"Cocksucker!" he said, and dove across the space between the two beds, his arms grabbing wildly.

Peter Pan was already airborne, hovering near the open window.

"Dirty son of a bitch!" Brinkley said; and lunged toward him.

Peter drifted out the window.

"Now, now, think Good Thoughts," he said.

Brinkley wanted to follow; to wring his neck. But he was too tired, too weak. He shook his fist at Peter. Peter only laughed, and waved; and disappeared over the roof.

Slowly, he closed the window, and straightened his uniform, and sat on the bed, bent over, his head in his hands.

"Creeping Cronkite," he said, now that his uniform was in place. "Of all things."

He felt dirtied, despoiled. Like some proper lady ending her days in a brothel.

Then he raised his head, hopefully; and stood, and went to the window. A bright morning sun was warming the city.

Jean Arthur, he was thinking. And Mary Martin. That's who played Peter on the stage. Maybe he wasn't a boy. Maybe he was a girl, after all. A slim, outrageous young girl, her beautiful blonde hair cut short . . .

Brinkley took a shower. When he emerged with a hotel towel around his waist, the phone between the two beds was ringing. It was Pamela.

"Hi, love," he said. "Where are you?"

"At the hospital."

"How's it coming?"

"Not it. David Junior. He's here."

"What? He's . . . when?"

"During the night. I couldn't reach you."

"I . . . David Junior? A boy?"

"Just like I promised."

"Oh, wow. Fantastic. Hey, listen. I'm sorry I wasn't there. I got hung up. Is everything okay?"

"Fine. I spoke to Mother. The kids are okay."

The towel was slipping from his waist. He grabbed at it.

"I mean you. How are you feeling?"

"Good. Except for a sore titty."

"You're out of practice."

"Practice, nothing. The baby has strong gums."

"You'll get used to it."

"Yeah, maybe. But I mean it about the little one. He's tough. You know when the doctor slapped him, to start him breathing?"

"Uh huh."

"The doctor sprained a finger."

"You're kidding. Poor old Sikes. Well, we paid him enough."

"Oh, I forgot to tell you. Sikes has the flu. He didn't do the delivery."

"Who did?"

"A young resident. Dr. Frankenplace. Or Frankenstein. Something like that."

Brinkley shuddered, without knowing why.

"Who does the baby look like?" he said.

"He's got my chin and eyes. And your hair."

"All thick and wavy?"

"No. Blue."

"Blue?"

"Uh huh."

"Is it awful?"

"Awful? He's beautiful!"

"With blue hair?"

"Just like yours."

The towel slipped from his waist again. He let it drop.

"Listen. . . . What time is it? I just got out of the shower. I'll put on some clothes and come right out."

"I'll be here."

"It won't take long. I love you."

"Pook?"

"What?"

"I love you, too."

"Mmmm . . ."

"Pook?"

"What?"

"Please don't rush. Take the train."

He blew a kiss into the phone, and hung up.

Take the train . . . ?

He dressed quickly. He called the office, to say he wouldn't be in. He packed his three uniforms in a box—the old one, the new one he had worn all night, the one Peter had left on the bed—and hurried to the elevator, and out into the street.

He hailed a cab.

"Where to?" Muhammad Ali said.

"Where's Bella?"

"Allah is everywhere. In your heart. In your mind . . ."

"Forget it. Penn Station, please."

As the cab floated through the streets, the city seemed to have returned to normal. The guardsmen and the barricades had been removed. Another crisis had been weathered, with scarcely a blink by the populace.

The last crisis he would ever solve.

He bought the paper, and settled onto the train. As it moved through the tunnels beneath the city, beneath the South River, he read Peggy's story. Under an eight-column headline, it told of how he had routed the muggers, and destroyed Elastic Man.

(There was nothing about Demoniac and Pxyzsyzygy. That she couldn't know.)

There was also an editorial on the front page, hailing his return.

He put the paper aside. Reading of his exploits, hearing the city once more singing his praises, filled him with nostalgia. With regret. Up in the Heavens, he could have heard all that again, throughout eternity. On Nudj. Or Bazoom. Or Wop. Or Kike. Or Nigger. Or Elvis.

The train emerged from the tunnel, into the sunshine of Swansdown Island. The trees in the backyards of private houses were clinging to their last autumn leaves: red, or brown, or gold.

In one yard, a man was tossing a football to his son. Teaching him how to catch it.

The train rushed on. The man was gone.

Brinkley closed his eyes, and leaned his head against the back of the seat. His arms rested lightly on the box of uniforms in his lap.

CPSIA information can be obtained
at www.ICGtesting.com
Printed in the USA
LVHW042319090419
613596LV00001B/35

9 780312 339920